LIFE HAPPENS NEXT

Also By Terry Trueman

Life Happens Next, 2012

Hurricane, 2008

7 Days at the Hot Corner, 2008

No Right Turn, 2006

Cruise Control, 2004

Inside Out, 2003

Stuck in Neutral, 2000

LIFE HAPPENS NEXT

Terry Trueman

HARPER TEEN
An Imprint of HarperCollinsPublishers

HarperTeen is an imprint of HarperCollins Publishers.

Life Happens Next
Copyright © 2012 by Terry Trueman
All rights reserved. Printed in the United States of America.
No part of this book may be used or reproduced in any manner whatsoever without
written permission except in the case of brief quotations embodied in critical articles
and reviews. For information address HarperCollins Children's Books, a division of
HarperCollins Publishers, 10 East 53rd Street, New York, NY 10022.
www.epicreads.com

Library of Congress Cataloging-in-Publication Data
Trueman, Terry.
    Life happens next / Terry Trueman. — 1st ed.
        p.   cm.
    Sequel to: Stuck in neutral.
    Summary: Shawn McDaniel, almost fifteen, cannot speak and has no control
over his body due to severe cerebral palsy, but he forms a strong connection with his
mother's cousin Debi, who has Down syndrome, and her dog Rusty.
    ISBN 978-0-06-202803-7 (trade bdg.)
    [1. Cerebral palsy—Fiction. 2. Down syndrome—Fiction. 3. People with
disabilities—Fiction. 4. Communication—Fiction. 5. Family life—Washington
(State)—Seattle—Fiction. 6. Dogs—Fiction. 7. Special education—Fiction.
8. Seattle (Wash.)—Fiction.] I. Title
PZ7.T7813 Lif 2012   2011044627
[Fic]—dc23   CIP
                                                                          AC

Typography by Michelle Gengaro-Kokmen
12 13 14 15 16   CG/RRDH   10 9 8 7 6 5 4 3 2 1
❖
First Edition

For Donna

LIFE HAPPENS NEXT

1

Night before last my dad tried to kill me. At least, I'm pretty sure that was his plan. For weeks and months I'd been worrying about it. I guess Dad had his reasons, but he didn't do it. Obviously. Lucky me, huh? Sorry, sarcasm is one of the few weapons I possess.

I heard this thing once on a TV program about a guy who had a recurring dream that he was a butterfly. One day he woke up and couldn't tell for sure if he was a butterfly dreaming he was a guy, or a guy dreaming he was a butterfly. Lately, when I first wake up, I have the feeling that maybe my dream life is better than my real life. Dreaming is my favorite part of each day, flying, soaring, feeling free because of all the amazing possibilities it offers. Yep, I've got reality—then everything else.

But here's the screwiest part: most of these dreamy possibilities spin around an impossible fact, the fact that I'm in love with Ally Williamson.

Damn, that's crazy. Maybe not so crazy for anybody else, but it sure is for me.

You see, I'm not exactly what you'd call red-hot, loverboy material. At least not on the outside. Actually, I'm pretty smart and funny—on the inside.

Confused? Okay, let's start with the facts. I'm Shawn McDaniel, and I have cerebral palsy. C.P. isn't always severe, but in my case it's about as bad as it can get. I am stuck in a wheelchair or on my bed 24/7. I wear diapers 'cause I can't use the toilet. I drool a lot so I often have a big bath towel tied around my neck soaked with spit. Between my diaper and my drool, are you surprised that I'm not exactly a sweet-smelling chick magnet? Hell, my own dad can barely stand to look at me. I go to a special program for school, a program just for kids like me. I know a lot of people call us "The Retards' Class"—nice, huh? My sister, Cindy, and brother, Paul, go to the same school, but my classes are totally separated. Separate but unequal.

Oh wait. There's more. I make loud sounds instead of words, incredibly irritating noises that I can't control. It's like my brain sends an order saying, "All right, Shawn, it's loud vocalizations time!" and a big fat "Ahhhhhhhh" jumps out of my mouth.

These vocalizations are as close as I ever get to communication with others, since I can't control ANY of my muscles at all.

It kills me that nobody knows I'm smart inside this useless shell. The people who love me most in the world, along with everybody else who ever sees me, think I'm a veg. I'm trapped inside my body.

So you see how this stuff makes it more than a little crazy for me to be in love? Especially with *the* most beautiful girl in the history of drop-dead-gorgeous girldom. Ally Williamson is Cindy's best friend, and while she knows I exist, that's the extent of our "relationship." In fact, the only time I get to see Ally is when my mom, Lindy, puts me in my regular spot in the family room, where Cindy and Ally usually hang out or watch TV. At these moments, I imagine Ally close to me. And lots of times my mind wanders into a daydream or fantasy. These are almost as good as my nighttime dreams, where Ally and I are walking on a deserted beach hand in hand, or running into the surf and diving into the blue waves or . . . never mind. The truth is that dreams and fantasies never last. Something like the breeze pressing against the windowpane, or some idiot on TV saying, "Love conquers all,"—something always snaps me out of it and back to reality.

"Love conquers all"?

Yeah, right. Maybe not quite *all*, huh?

I've been in love with Ally Williamson from the first second I ever saw her. Love at first sight. Well, maybe not the exact first second but pretty freakin' close to it. One night she came to our house for a sleepover with my sister and I got to hang out with them. Okay, "hang out with them" is not quite accurate. I got to sit in my wheelchair, little more than a lump of human flesh and unacknowledged teenaged horniness, in the room next to where they were. But at that first meeting Ally greeted me, looking right into my eyes. She was warm and kind, which caught me off guard. Hardly anybody ever acts interested when they are introduced to me, probably because all I do is sit and drool back at them, but Ally spoke to me. Her voice was a little too loud, which was probably nervousness, but there was nothing phony in her tone or words. I mean it was like she didn't even see my wheelchair or smell my ugly scent or judge me in any way. She was nice and, yep, totally gorgeous, so I admit that this combination of kindness and gorgeousness gave me the absolute, total, over-the-top, teenaged-love-junkie, mac-daddy-extreme *hotz* for her.

When I got put to bed later that night, I tossed and turned. I guess I should say that my brain tossed and turned me, thinking about Ally, her smile, eyes, lips, hair, her slender hands that cradled my face and brushed my cheek when she said good night. Okay, to be honest, I made up that last part.

But when I finally fell asleep, I had this wonderful dream, where we were kissing and cuddling. And in the dream, Ally looked me in the eyes and told me she loved me. I told her I loved her too, knowing somehow that this was true not just in my dream but in reality, also.

Now I am consumed by wanting to know her and to be known by her, to love and be loved. In the dream, I felt that I *had* to be known and loved by her—*I had to be!* When I woke up in the morning, I started to worry. How can that ever happen? The reality is there is no way I can *ever* tell Ally how I really feel. And it hurts because without being loved for who you really are, without being known by anybody, what does life even mean?

I've had cerebral palsy from birth, and never being "normal," I've had to adjust to a lot of things that most people don't even consider. If you think about the phrase "take it for granted" and then think about all the stuff normal people do all the time, it's amazing: walking, talking, peeing, winking, sighing, crying, burping, farting, laughing, staring, grabbing, holding, kissing, blushing. Do normal people ever think of any of these things as amazing? I doubt it. Not having any control over any of my body's parts, not being able to tell my hand, "pick up that cup," or tell my eyes, "blink, yeah that was fun, now let's blink again," makes normal things seem pretty awesome to me.

But I've gotten used to not being able to do all those things that normal people do all the time. What I'm never going to be able to get used to is dreaming about Ally Williamson, kissing her in my dreams (I *love* these dreams), loving her, and then waking up and realizing it will never be real, that these dreams will never come true.

So now you get that my body doesn't work. But my brain sure does. I'm almost fifteen years old, and since thinking is about all I can do, I've done a lot of it in my day. The only thing I can do to keep myself from getting depressed is just stay cool. I once heard my sister say to Paul, "No situation is so bad that having a bad attitude can't make it worse." I love that. My situation is pretty bad, but I've got my hopes and dreams and firm belief that life is a pretty great thing. And thinking about Ally, fantasizing that we might some-how be together someday, is more than enough of a reason for me to live.

So back to my dad and how he planned to kill me a couple nights ago. He actually thought he'd be doing me a favor, ending my miserable existence. But because Dad didn't do it, I guess in one way I'm like everybody else now, just try-ing to figure out what's gonna happen next. I'm keeping my spirits up and enjoying a mental make-out here and there (hey, it's better than no make-out at all!), and focusing on the good things in life. Yeah, I've got C.P. but I know that there's always bad and good things coming at us that we can't even see, much less control. So how different am I from everyone else? Maybe not so much as it looks like.

2

Here's how I spin things in my head—some cool things about being me:

1. I get a hot bath every day of my life and never have to lift a finger. The warm water gets squeezed over my body from the big sponge in my mom's gentle, loving hands. And this bath is by far the most enjoyable physical sensation I ever feel.
2. I have a perfect auditory memory, remembering *everything* I *ever* hear, which is *totally* cool. This ability has turned our TVs (and we have four of them!) into the greatest learning devices in the universe. I mean, who needs real life when you've got 110 cable stations? And I remember *every* show, from Cesar Millan's *The Dog Whisperer* to Little

League baseball to the love life of squids to "The bark beetle lays its eggs" to everything in between. In other words, I'm damned smart!

3. Although I can't tell anybody what kind of music I'd like to listen to, I love almost all the music that's played around here (rap/hip-hop, R&B, Bach and Mozart, geezer R&R) so whatever's on pretty much always makes me happy.

4. My brother, Paul, King Jock, Straight-A Student, Tough Guy Supreme, slips me bites of his deluxe bacon double cheeseburgers every chance he gets. Somehow Paul knows that I, too, think God invented this food to make up for the fact that all of us have to die someday.

5. My sister, Cindy, is a saint. She taught me to read by playing school with me when I was little, and to this day she never treats me bad—plus she has *great* taste in best friends, *wink-wink-hubba-hubba!*

6. Although Mom has a master's degree in English and could be a college teacher or have some other higher-paying job, she works from home so she can take care of me. If Cindy is a saint, think about what that makes my mom.

7. I'll never have to get a lousy part-time job like carrying people's groceries to their cars in a supermarket parking lot or cleaning out toilets and

mopping floors in some crummy restaurant.

8. In fact, I'll never have to get *any* job, which I figure is a good thing since *work* is a four-letter word . . .

9. . . . so I'll never have anybody bossing me around—I know this is partly a bad thing as I'll never get to boss anybody else either, but I don't think I'd like doing that anyway.

10. I have a kickass name. Shawn McDaniel is really cool sounding when compared to a name like Elmer Ulysses Fudpucker or Isaac P. Freeley.

11. I'm living in the most interesting time in all of history: medical science–wise, it is a miracle that a guy like me, with my so-called handicaps, could still even be alive.

Okay, let's make this 12 items:

12. I am in love with Ally Williamson, the girl of my dreams, and while I'd love to find some way to make her fall in love with me too, at least I get to imagine that she's mine all mine.

Ah, what the heck, just for good luck let's make it 13. I didn't even mention my dream life yet. Did I say dream life? Hey, Ally, here I come!

3

Last night I had another dream about Ally. I was flying; soaring is more like it. I do this a lot in dreams and also when I have seizures. That's when my spirit escapes my body and I'm no longer trapped, not limited, not so isolated. That's why I don't mind my seizures, even though I know, from hearing my family talk, that when I'm having one it looks like I'm being tortured to death. When you live in a body with zero control, escaping it, even if it's when you're asleep or having a grand mal seizure, is great.

When I have a seizure, I am released from the crippling constraints of my useless body. Time and space have no control over me. Neither does gravity or any other "real" things like walls, fences, concrete, wood, asphalt, steel bars. Nothing can keep me from going where I want to go or hold me back at all. But sometimes during seizures, and like in this dream, I don't choose a destination. It's more like a destination chooses me.

In my dream last night, I was coasting over Puget Sound, its dark water shimmering in bright moonlight, sea birds flying by my side, their black eyes staring into my eyes. After a while I shot up toward the stars. Then I swooped down and could see the lights of people's houses and streetlamps. I spotted my house and dived back.

Now it was daylight. I saw Ally sitting in our living room. She looked up and saw me. I paused, still floating outside the window. She smiled at me. And she spoke without words, her thoughts coming through loud and clear: "Shawn, I love you."

Suddenly I was standing up tall and strong on my own two feet. And Ally came running out of the house, all slow motion, jiggling in just the right places and smiling wide. She was unbelievably happy and beautiful.

"I'm ready to go!" she said. I turned around and there was a gorgeous red Corvette waiting for us in the driveway. We settled into the leather bucket seats and Ally puckered her lips and threw me a kiss. That kiss floated through space toward my cheek and I power-shifted the 'vette, banging it hard from second into third, like a hotrod king in a video game, like a NASCAR wild man defying death. My engine screamed, Ally purred, and I . . .

. . . woke up. Lying in my crib with a wet diaper and a

deep longing to be back in my dream—back where Ally and I were together. If I could have squeezed my eyes tight to make it happen, I'd have done it in a heartbeat—but I can't control my eyelids any more than I can control *any* part of my body.

So what I love about dreams and seizures is that I'm in control in my travels and my spirit is free. I mean how could I *not* have mixed emotions about returning to my body? I know I should be thankful for still being alive and all, but I always feel sad that my travels and adventures are over. This morning it was hard to wake up and realize that Ally doesn't love me. My only choice was to launch into a daydream to avoid the reality of my growing diaper rash.

Like most boys, my best daydreams are R-rated—R for restricted audience, no one under 17 allowed. In this morning's daydream, I went to Ally's house or what I thought her house might look like. I have no idea how I knew where it was, but in daydreams you just know stuff. Somehow I knew where her room was too. I peeked in and saw her single bed already made, her closet door ajar, filled with tops and jeans, flannels and hoodies and jackets, her shoes stacked on a shoe rack.

I heard a shower running and couldn't resist moving toward the bathroom at the end of the hallway. Light shone from below the closed bathroom door with a tiny bit of steam. I felt the warmth of the room, the moist air even before I got to the door and paused.

I knew for sure that it was Ally showering. From outside I could feel her presence. Then it was like Ally could also tell I was there. "Come join me, Shawn. After all, we're in love, aren't we?"

I've never actually had a shower in my life. Like I mentioned before, my mom bathes me, but I can't be left alone for even a second in a bathtub, because if I had a seizure or even just fell over, I'd drown. But in the daydream we were in the shower together, and it seemed as though Ally and I had been like this many times before. It was completely natural. Like I said, this dream is R-rated, so I won't go into all the details. We were just two people in the shower together and the girl was really, really *hot*, so you do the math.

The downside was leaving my daydream. I wanted to stay where I had been, longed to keep feeling the warm water and Ally's touch lingering . . . sigh . . . and you wonder why I like dreams so much?

4

Dreaming is one thing. Reality is something else. Like every Monday through Friday morning, I'm at school. And like most every other day, I've just made a mess in my diaper. You might think I'd get used to this since I've never used a toilet in my life, but I hate it. It's not like I have any choice in the matter. I know when I need to go, either number one or number two, and I wish I could just say, "Excuse me please, I need to use the bathroom." But I can't. I can't say anything. I can't tap my foot, or make my eyes blink, or wiggle my pinky as a signal to get me to the john. I can't push a button on a communication board or make myself say "Ahhhhhh" as a signal. I can't do anything except, well, just let it happen and wait for someone to check me out or to notice the smell and say, "Shawn needs changing."

I don't feel humiliation, exactly, or embarrassment

since there's nothing I can do to change the situation, but I always feel sad and sorry for whoever it is who changes me. And at school that job usually goes to the teacher's aide, William.

"Okay, buddy," William says as he lifts me from my wheelchair and helps me walk. I always say I can't walk, but if someone holds me under my arms, like William is doing right now, and kind of carries me along, my legs will move one foot after another until William lowers me to the floor into a kneeling position. Now I can stay upright and rock back and forth. This is funny because I don't do this by choice; my body just rocks back and forth and I can't stop it any more than start it—it just happens.

William rolls me onto my back, sort of gently lifting me by my legs so whatever size mess is in my diaper doesn't get all mashed up even worse than it already is and spread around. He unsnaps the legs on my pants. He lifts my pant legs up and out of the way and undoes my disposable diaper by tearing the little taped fasteners, folds it over on itself, and sets it aside. Using a handy wipe from a big plastic tub next to the changing blanket, he wipes me until I'm clean. He's never rough or in a hurry. Now he puts another diaper on me, snug but not too tight.

"That feel better?" he almost always asks.

I think back to him, "Yeah, thank you, William—I feel really bad you have to do this."

And sometimes, like now, I wonder if he thinks back to me, "No problem, Shawn—you're a good kid and you can't help it."

Truthfully, I kind of doubt that William thinks this, but his kindness makes me realize that he really does care about me.

This whole diaper-changing thing also makes me wonder about the huge difference between kindness and meanness. Think about it—I don't have all that many interactions with people, I'm mostly just sort of "handled," more of a problem than a person. William could be a total dick toward me, but he never is. Seems to me there are a million examples of how nice or how cruel people act every moment of every day. The way William so patiently and tenderly helps me is a great example of kindness. But meanness is always about half an inch away too. Life is such a jumbled mess of good and bad and totally random things, like having C.P. or not having it. William is kind, for no real reason, he just is that way. Other people, not so much.

This morning, for example, Mom was driving me to school like she always does in our special handicap-equipped van. Our house is on Queen Anne Hill, and the road leading down the hill from our place is winding and two lanes, one lane in each direction. There are a couple signs that read 30 MPH, but Mom takes some of the curves slower, probably thinking about me in my wheelchair bolted behind her and not wanting to toss me around too much.

I only caught a brief glimpse of a guy in a black pickup truck trailing us. With my eyes, a glimpse is all I usually catch of *anything*, so I've learned to observe as much as I can. The guy driving the truck looked middle-aged. He had a mustache and a baseball cap, a cigarette hanging from his lips. He was tailgating us, no more than a couple feet off our back bumper. I couldn't tell if Mom noticed him or not.

At the bottom of the hill, there's a bank with a parking lot that has driveway entries and exits coming off both the road we were on and the main arterial ahead of us. My focus had shifted away from the side mirror and the truck by then. I wouldn't have given it another thought at all if I hadn't been suddenly startled by the roar of his incredibly loud horn blast, no little beep-beep, but a sustained HOOONNNNNKKK! This sound caused my brain to shift my head in its direction and my legs and arms to twitch and flail around.

The black truck raced into the bank's parking lot, its horn still blaring, and then I saw the driver lean forward and give mom a dirty look and the middle finger salute. It was like he thought she'd committed some huge crime against him by driving carefully down the hill. On the truck's back bumper were a couple stickers: MY KID CAN BEAT UP YOUR HONOR STUDENT and KEEP YOUR HANDS OFF MY LIBERTY. And in the rear window of the truck's cab there was a cartoon of a little boy peeing and staring backward over his shoulder with a nasty snarly smile. The truck bounced pretty hard, as if it were in a four-wheel, cross-country rally on TV. It shot through the parking lot and roared out onto the arterial, forcing several other cars to brake to avoid him.

Everything happened so fast. But when I finally managed to catch a glimpse of Mom, her face reflected in the rearview mirror of the van, she appeared calm and relaxed, as if nothing had happened. Not me, though. I felt tense and mad. I remembered a line I heard once in a movie where the good guy gets angry at someone and says of him, "I wish him ill." In my own road rage toward that guy in the black pickup truck, I wished him ill every bit as much as I wish good things in life for William, my primary diaper-changer. I'm no perfect little angel, that's for sure—I mean, would a perfect little angel wish that he could jump up out of his wheelchair, tear his T-shirt off like some steroid-addled wrestle-mania villain, and rip that jerkwad's lungs out? I'm just a kid who once in a while wishes his life could be different than it is and who knows that wishes don't change things all the time—or *any of the time* for some stuff.

5

It's the next day, early afternoon. The front door to our house flies open and Paul bursts through. "Hey!" he yells. He's in a great mood. A few days ago his hoops team won the state championship and he was the MVP of the game and he's still riding high. Paul comes into the family room where Cindy and Ally sit, pausing only long enough to get a kiss on the cheek from Mom, who is in the kitchen. Cindy jumps up and gives him a high five. He walks over to me sitting in my wheelchair and messes up my hair. "Hey bro," he says. With his fingers he combs my hair back into place.

Something is different about Paul lately. I can't say exactly what it is, but for a long time he's been so angry with our dad in particular and the world in general. I know from what I've overheard that Paul has been in a lot of

20

fights—and I've seen him lose his temper more than once. It's *not* a pretty sight. But in the past few weeks, his anger seems to have lessened. I'm glad for him. He's always been an amazing brother, protective and kind. I love him.

He loves me a lot too. And he's proved it in the most important ways. My brother saved my life even though he doesn't know it. Paul phoned from Spokane just a few minutes after they won their basketball game, the night I was talking about before, the night that my dad planned to "end my pain." Paul had wanted to share the moment with me. Dad was leaning over me, a pillow in his hands, when the phone rang. Dad answered. He and Paul talked. I was out of my body in a seizure during most of their conversation, but when I got back from my seizure, I heard Dad say, "I'll tell him, Paul, I promise."

When he hung up the phone, Dad's face was covered in tears and he said to me, "Your brother asked me to tell you that he dedicated his game to you—and that he loves you." Then Dad stood and leaned over me in my crib, tossed the pillow away, and pulled my blankets back up to my neck. He whispered, "You sleep now, Shawn. Sweet dreams." And he walked quietly out of my bedroom, closing the door behind him. That was the end of my worries about Dad putting an end to my pain. And it was also the beginning of the rest of my life.

* * *

Today I watch Paul and Ally make eye contact. Neither says a word but both smile and blush. A long pause. Paul finally says, "Hi, Ally."

She says, "Hi . . . ," pausing a moment longer, then adding, "Congratulations." More blushing. They keep staring at each other.

In an instant my heart breaks into about a thousand pieces. I feel tears come to my eyes, totally involuntary tears since I can't make myself cry any more than I can make myself not cry. My breathing, also out of my control, starts to speed along with my racing heartbeat. Sweat pours down my armpits and covers my forehead and temples. Ally Williamson, the girl I love more than anybody in the world, the girl I fantasize might someday love me in return, is going to be with my brother.

Paul is a great athlete—muscular and tough and brave, the kind of guy every guy envies, the kind of guy every girl dreams about. And even though I love Ally, want her, desperately obsess about her, and even though I noticed her first, Paul has no way of knowing how I feel. It's pretty obvious Ally likes him too. How can I fantasize about Ally if she's gonna be with Paul?

Man, no kidding, could life suck any worse than this? Seriously, if I can't fantasize about loving Ally, if I can't even *hope* and *dream* of it, what's the point in being alive? And really, as long as guys like Paul are around, how can somebody like me ever hope to connect with anybody, not just Ally but with *anyone*? Maybe when my dad was thinking about "ending my pain," he had the right idea, even if he doesn't have a clue what real pain is for me.

Okay, I know, here I am, the Heartbreak Retard running wild. But I don't care. Hey! For the first time, I feel like every other teen with a broken heart—baaaaaddddd!

6

It's been eight days since Ally and Paul got together—the eight worst, most self-pitying-pathetic-little-me days of my entire life. What started with blushing and staring into each other's eyes like a teen couple in one of those dreadful Lifetime (should be called Lifelong) TV movies has kept marching right along for Paul and Ally. Every stinking day.

A big difference for me between being in love and being brokenhearted is that nothing changes in my world except for how I feel. I can't get up and walk around depressed, or break stuff, or give killer stares to total strangers just because they're too happy or something. My hopeless inability to connect with others in any way isn't true only of love and lost love; it's true of *everything* for me. When something terrible happens, I can't scream obscenities, or cut myself, or throw myself off the Space Needle. Things happen in my life, like in everybody else's, but I can't do anything about it, including telling anyone how I feel.

I could stand to blow off a little steam right now, especially since life is smacking me down pretty bad this week. Can't a gimped-out kid catch a break? Today Mom and Cindy and I went into the pharmacy to pick up my anti-seizure medicine. Mom went off to shop for a few more things, and Cindy was rolling me down an aisle in my wheelchair. I started vocalizing really loudly.

A big lady in a floral dress came around to see what all the commotion was about. I *am* awfully loud, but the look on that lady's face when she saw me, the revulsion in her eyes, was malignant. Cindy's hands shook on the handles of my wheelchair, bad enough so I could feel it. The woman couldn't tear her eyes away, like I was one of the fifty-cent sideshows at an old-time circus, Two-Ton Tony or The Bearded Lady or Shawn the Ahhhhhh Freak.

Cindy snapped at the woman who was staring, "Yo, take a picture, it'll last longer!" shooting laser death glares at her.

The lady went beet red, turned on her heel, and left.

Cindy came around and knelt in front of me and took my hands in hers. Her hands still quivered, and she started sobbing. She had to take deep breaths before she could even speak. Some snot was running out of her nose and she kept sniffing. Finally Cindy let go of one of my hands and wiped her nose with the back of her hand.

"Don't pay attention to her, Shawn," she said, her voice soft and shaking, pausing and taking a couple deep breaths. "Don't think about her."

Much as I love my sister, I knew that Cindy wasn't talking to me; she was talking to herself. And I knew that she felt terrible, an ugly mix of embarrassed, pissed, and helpless. To tell the truth, I felt that way too.

7

One thing about Mom is the way she always stays positive. She is feeding me lumpy cottage cheese mixed with applesauce. As she gently scrapes the edge of the spoon up my chin to capture the escaping food drool, she says, "Are you as excited as I am about Debi and Rusty coming to live with us?"

And who, you may wonder, are these "exciting" new roomies, Debi and Rusty?

Debi Eagen is a forty-one-year-old woman with Down syndrome, a genetic condition that makes a person developmentally disabled or, if you're into labels, "retarded."

By the way, about this word, *retard*, and my just saying it, I know that often people call someone a "retard" in a teasing way. Other times they say it to be cruel. It's just a word. The folks who get most mad about it are the people in our lives who care for us and love us and want to protect us. It's not us retards ourselves. Heck, we know what we are.

But the way I see it is this: if African American rappers want to call themselves by the "n" word, they can. And if people from any ethnic, religious, racial, sexual orientation, or *any* group, get to use the slang of their choice to describe themselves, then we people who are labeled developmentally disabled can sure as hell use the "r" word if we want to. Makes sense, right?

So Debi is a retard, like me. And like most people with Down syndrome, she's slow but not helpless, or nearly as bad off as I appear to be. She may have the mental age of a four- or five-year-old kid, but she can do some things for herself, and compared to what I *can't* do, well, there's no comparison.

Many folks with Down are pretty active. On weekdays Debi goes to the North Neighborhood Community Center's Learning Skills Program. Mom tried to get me into weekend activities there once, but it's an adults-only program, plus you have to be able to use the bathroom on your own. No way. I'm a kid, not an "adults-only," and potty training isn't exactly in my immediate future (okay, it ain't even in my *distant* future), so the weekend thing didn't work out for me. But Debi will be going there Mondays through Fridays.

Rusty is coming to live with us too. But fear not, our house isn't being overrun by a sudden attack of D.D. hordes. Rusty's not developmentally disabled. In fact, Rusty's not even human: Vampire? Zombie? Devil or angel? Nope, not even close. Rusty is a dog.

So why are Debi and Rusty moving in with us? Debi is Mom's cousin; her parents are my mom's aunt and uncle—well, they *were* anyway. Seven years ago Debi's mother died from Alzheimer's. Debi's dad passed away last month, leaving Debi with no one to take care of her. Maybe everybody thought, since my mom already has one retard, why not give her another? I know that sounds harsh, but I think it's true, at least partly true. Probably the bigger reason that Mom stepped up, though, is that there was no one else to take care of Debi, much less her dog.

We have two extra bedrooms in our daylight basement area that is almost like an apartment by itself, plenty of space for Debi and Rusty. Mom's question, am I excited about Debi and Rusty moving in?—well, I guess I'm a tiny bit excited, maybe more like curious, about what it will be like to have Debi living with us. As for Rusty, not so much.

I heard Mom describing Rusty to Cindy and Paul as being "excitable," but since she also said that he bites people, I think that's a mild way of putting it. Excited? About a killer canine that bites people? Like I said, not exactly.

8

I'm parked at my usual place by the window when Debi and Mrs. Pearson, the social worker from the nursing home where Debi's been living, arrive to check out our place.

Mom says, "Hi, Debi."

Debi answers, "I like McDonnos."

Mom glances at Mrs. Pearson, who says *"McDonald's. She likes McDonald's. She says that a lot."*

Debi interjects, "I want go dare now."

"After our visit, Debi," Mrs. Pearson says. "Remember, we're here to see your cousin Lindy."

Debi blinks and looks at Mom, then nods. "Yeth," she says softly.

Mom says "hi" again and Debi answers "hi" back.

My brain picks this moment to vocalize, so I chip in a

loud "Ahhhhhh." Hey, always glad to be part of the fun, right?

Debi looks over at me and asks, "Who dat boy?"

Mom answers, "That's my son Shawn. Would you like to meet him?"

"No," Debi answers, perfectly clear.

"Maybe later," Mom says.

"No tanks," Debi says.

I'm cool with Debi not wanting to meet me. I like that she's so honest. I mean let's face it, I'm a little weird looking, sitting here like an idiot.

Mom says, "Shawn's going to stay here while I show you your room, Debi. Follow me."

Mom leads Mrs. Pearson and Debi down the curving, circular stairway.

I hear them some, not real clearly, in the basement, their voices carrying up the stairs.

Mom: "Do you think you'll like it here, Debi?"

Debi: ". . . mumble-mumble . . . McDonnos."

Mrs. Pearson: "Yes, Debi, McDonald's is good. Do you like your room? It's a nice room, huh?"

Debi: "Yeth. I like. Rusty have a bed too?"

Mom: "Sure, Debi, Rusty will be welcome."

When they come back upstairs, Mom and Mrs. Pearson shake hands. Mrs. Pearson says, "I'm sure there'll be no problem whatsoever. I'll sign off for her things to be delivered tomorrow, and she'll be able to come the day after."

"That's fine," Mom says.

As Debi and Mrs. Pearson start walking toward the front door, Mom nods at me. "Debi," she says, "my son's name is Shawn. You can meet him next time you come, okay?"

Debi looks back at me and stutters. "S-S-S . . . Swan."

Mom smiles. "Close enough."

Before I can stop my smart-ass mind, I think, "Duh-Duh-Duh . . . Debi."

Come on, Shawn, knock it off! I'd kick myself if I could, for making fun of her, but I think, still sarcastically imitating Debi's voice, "Tanks a lot, Mom." Why am I acting like a spoiled pea brain? I'm probably just jealous. After all, I almost never get to visit McDonno . . . I mean, McDonald's.

9

Yesterday Debi moved in. She had dinner with us, and then she went off to bed.

She comes out of her room this morning ready to go to what she calls "schoo," dressed in a Winnie the Pooh sweatshirt, bright yellow pants with a fire-engine-red cowboy hat perched on her head, maybe five sizes too small.

Paul smiles at her and says, "Howdy, Tex."

Debi answers "howdy" right back.

Paul asks, "You rustling cattle out on the ranch?"

Debi smiles. "You funny, B-B-B-Baul. You should be comedy man."

My reaction to her wardrobe is a little less charitable than my brother's. I'd like to say to Debi, "As a person with Down syndrome already, overweight, stubby, obviously a couple sandwiches short of a picnic, could you possibly make yourself look any more ridiculous?"

After Debi's bus arrives to take her to the Learning Skills Program, Paul and Mom talk in the kitchen before he leaves for school.

Paul says, "I'm thinking a little bit about Stanford, more as a baseball school than for football or hoops."

Mom answers, "It's a great school."

Paul starts saying, "I know it's expensive but—"

Mom interrupts. "Wherever you decide to go, sweetie, you know your dad and I will do all we can to help. We're both so proud of you."

After another mind-numbing school day, Mom picks me up and parks me by the window. It's not raining today, and in Seattle at this time of year, that's a minimiracle. Plus the sun is out and there is no wind to speak of, just a soft breeze. I can see the willow and locust trees in our yard, their little leaves mostly motionless and the sun shining on them. A few clouds, puffy, like cotton balls, sit in the bright blue sky. It's almost spring. But I have a hard time feeling very happy about it.

I'm thinking about Mom and Paul's conversation from this morning. I guess I'm feeling torn. Torn between pride for all my brother's accomplishments and for all the opportunities they are bringing him, but I feel angry too. I try to bring myself back to that positive place where I can remember a few good things about my life, but I can't. All I can think of is why? Why couldn't I have gotten just some of the things he's got—legs that run, an arm that throws, a girl like Ally? Heck, *any* girl.

I can't seem to shake these thoughts as I hang around waiting for Paul and Cindy to get home from school. But before I know it, it's that time. Paul is the first one home.

After letting a bunch of bitterness rise up in me today— today? Let's be honest, for *many* days—if there was any hope of seeing Paul and letting my pride and love for him take over, that hope is squashed when Ally walks in with him, her arm woven around my brother's arm, like some kind of ridiculous flesh pretzel, their hands touching.

Paul whispers something to her, too soft for me to hear. Ally laughs and pulls her arm away from him and punches his shoulder. He laughs too.

"Hi, kids," Mom says.

Both Ally and Paul say "hi" together, and look at each other and laugh. What's so funny about saying "hi" at the same time? I'll tell you what. *Nothing.*

Mom gets up and says, "I'm gonna go up to my room and work. If you need anything, just holler."

Paul says to Mom, "We'll keep an eye on Shawn."

Mom, already walking toward the upstairs staircase,

says, "Thanks, kids, that'd be great."

Paul asks Ally, "You hungry?"

Ally answers, "No, I'm fine. I had three tacos for lunch."

Paul teases, "Pretty girl, count calories much?"

Ally answers, "Pretty boy, who is eating two hours after lunch and an hour before dinner?"

"Touché," Paul says, going to the pantry while Ally takes a seat behind the countertop.

I'm stuck here listening to this lovey-dovey bull-pucky. It's like they're an old married couple already, kidding around, so comfortable with each other. My head shifts and I'm facing Ally's direction. I can't will myself to turn my head, but once in a while, it moves where I want it to look and sometimes, like now, it moves where I kind of wish it wouldn't.

I see Ally, not all of her, just her head and shoulders over the top of the counter, in profile to me, like a cameo—perfect and lovely. My heart jumps and sinks all at once. Her hair, long and light brown, shines in the sunlight pouring in through the kitchen window. Her skin is so smooth, it looks like alabaster or pearl. Her expression matches the sound of her voice, happy and relaxed.

Now I see Paul, who walks toward the counter from the fridge, carrying a jar of mayonnaise, a packet of lunch meat and cheese, some mustard, a tiny jar of creamy horse-radish sauce, and a loaf of bread. He balances all of it so easily, without any effort, as he unloads each item onto the counter. He's soooo Mr. Cool, soooo Mr. Perfect.

If I could speak, what would I say? "Hey, Ally, I know Paul is a great athlete, but I have perfect auditory memory and remember everything I've heard, so I'll bet I'm way smarter than him." As it happens, though, Paul gets straight As in school. He's no slouch himself. Plus he's in advanced college prep classes while I'm in special education where, despite the hardworking educational staff, I haven't been able to repeat one single word back to them, or learn how to use the toilet or how to tie my shoes. Maybe comparing my intellectual achievements to my brother's would not be the best way to go. So maybe I'd say, "Hey, Ally, no one could ever love you as much as me, I guarantee it. I mean think about it, if you loved me half as much as I love you, I'd never take it for granted." But is this the kind of "love" Ally, or any girl, wants? "Love" from a guy in a wheelchair who everybody in the world thinks is a total imbecile, worshiping her but unable to do anything to prove it?

I watch them both more closely. I hate to admit it, but they're so perfect for each other. More perfect, even, than Ally and I ever seemed to be in my best dreams about us. She's gorgeous. He's handsome. She's a bit quiet and serious and shy. He's confident and strong and bold. She can help Paul control his anger and temper. He can help her learn to have fun and take a few risks. I mean they are like every perfect couple you ever see in movies and on TV shows. The way they balance each other out, they'll be better people for it. Excuse me, can anyone please direct me to the nearest vomitorium?

As I'm thinking all this negative crap, I overhear Ally say to Paul, "I can't wait to meet Debi."

Paul laughs and says, "Yeah, she's a trip all right."

Now Ally pauses a few seconds before saying, "I think it will be neat for Shawn to have a friend like Debi."

Paul says, "You think?"

Ally sounds so sincere. "Absolutely, having someone who is more like him, a companion who's more on his level. I'm so happy for him."

What!

Oh, man!

Debi and *me*? Is that Ally's idea of a great match? Debi is a forty-one-year-old, five-foot-two, eyes-of-blue, 220-pound lady with Down syndrome and the mind of a five-year-old. And I am, by all outward appearances, the drooling fourteen-year-old idiot in the wheelchair wearing a diaper. Sounds to me like a marriage made in developmental disability hell.

If I could talk, I'd scream, "Damn it Ally, it's you I want!" If I could grab a butcher knife, I'd slit my throat. If I could get myself to the top of the Space Needle, I'd take a header down to the concrete, seven hundred feet below. But of course I can't do any of these things. All I can do is sit here and, against all odds, actually feel worse than I did ten minutes ago.

10

A couple more miserable days have dragged by. It's almost 7:30 in the evening. Dinner is over. Cindy and Paul are upstairs in their bedrooms, supposedly "studying" although I hear a lot of music clashing up there, Mozart from Cindy's room and hip-hop from Paul's. Mom is still messing around in the kitchen.

Debi is sitting in the family room staring at me. And I mean *staring*. I never see her blink even once. It seems like Debi is trying to figure something out. Her focus is amazing. But I'm not sure if it's intentional or just random staring, whether I am in her thoughts or if she is in some sort of strange blank zone. It makes me wonder, what's up with her?

After about half an hour of this weird gawking, Mom comes into the living room and says, "Hi, Debi."

Debi's concentration breaks. She looks at Mom and answers, "Dat's my name, don't wear it out," and laughs.

Mom laughs too and now reminds Debi that her dog is coming tonight.

Debi looks at Mom and says, "Yeth, Wusty," turns, and walks into the foyer and plops herself down on the bench in front of the door.

Thirty minutes later a car pulls into the driveway.

Debi yells, "Wusty's here!" My mother helps her unlock the door.

"WUSTY!" Debi yells.

I hear a growl and a ripping sound and now a man's voice. "Gosh," he says apologetically, "Sorry about your screen door."

Mom quickly answers, "That's all right, it needed replacing anyway—"

Her words are cut off as Rusty tears into the house, claws clattering on the hardwood, whining and barking like a maniac. I can barely even make out the thump of Paul's feet hitting the stairs as he comes to see what all the commotion is about, or his voice calling over the chaos, "This must be Rusty!"

The man says loudly to Paul, "I wouldn't pet him until he has a chance to—" He stops in midsentence, and I hear Paul's voice, "Rusty boy, who that good boy?"

The man speaks again. "Wow, he seems to like you."

I can hear Rusty's collar jingling and tail thumping on the hardwood. Paul laughs, slapping the dog's sides and talking to him. "Who that good boy? You that Rusty boy!"

Mom says, "Hi, Rusty." And now, again, the sound of the dog's claws as they clatter, scratch, and claw over the floor in his effort to run.

Debi cries, "WUSTY, SIT."

But I can tell by the noise that he's sure not sitting.

The man says, "Calm down, Rusty," but the dog seems to ignore him, too. The man explains, "He's a smart dog, but he's got a bit of nervous aggression and doesn't take to new environments or new people all that well." He adds, "I'm surprised he likes this young man so much."

Mom says, "My son Paul."

The man says, "Jack Yurrik. Nice to meet you both."

Paul answers, "Nice to meet you, too."

"WUSTY," Debi cries again, and now the sound of Rusty's claws grows closer to me.

I happen to be staring down toward the floor at the foot of my wheelchair when I hear a loud, angry bark. I've watched enough *Dog Whisperer* episodes to know that this bark sounds different than the dog's excitement of a few moments ago. This barking is angry, scared, and is followed by a low, deep growl, a clear warning sound. Suddenly my wheelchair jerks. The growling sound is right next to me.

My body tenses up involuntarily.

"No! Rusty!" the man yells.

Mom hurries to my side and tries to shoo Rusty away.

I hear Paul, close by, laugh and say, "Never seen a wheel-chair before huh, buddy?"

"Be careful," the man says as I feel my wheelchair jerk again.

But Paul speaks calmly and firmly to Rusty. "It's okay, buddy," he says, almost whispering, "Sit. See? It's okay. We don't bite wheelchair wheels around here. Just sit and stay."

I'm so rattled that I'm shaking, and I realize Rusty can't control his fear any more than I can control mine. It's kind of a downer to realize that I have so much in common with a dog.

Sarcastically I think, "Welcome to my world, Rusty."

11

The phone rings and Mom picks it up. After saying hello, she says, "Hi, Syd."

It's my dad calling. My dad is the poet Sydney McDaniel, author of the Pulitzer Prize–winning book *Shawn,* his version of our lives, of *my* life with him. *Shawn* tells the story of what he went through after I was born brain injured. The book made him rich and famous.

I see the tension in Mom's face as she listens to him, and I hear how uptight she is when she replies, "No, Debi moving in isn't about the money—"

Dad must have interrupted, because Mom gets quiet.

Now Mom says, "No, honestly, we're doing fine. We're giving this thing with Debi a trial run to see how it works—"

She listens a moment and answers, "Yes, of course Paul

and Cindy agreed—"

Another pause. "Well, the dog *is* a handful, but Paul seems to have his number already."

A laugh from Mom. "No, you're right, Debi's not exactly a great dog trainer."

They talk for another few minutes and finally Mom says, "Okay, see you then." She hangs up the phone.

Hearing Mom talking to Dad reminds me that I hardly think about his mercy-killing plan anymore. It's not that this wasn't important to me, but now that I don't have death hanging over me, I have so many other things on my mind.

I suppose if you are a normal person, a person who takes everything about your normalcy for granted, it would be impossible to understand how a guy like me feels about life in general and my life in particular. The truth is that I've been mostly happy. But since that near-death thing with Dad, I've also wondered, what does my life mean? Being brain injured the way I am, unable to walk, talk, or communicate in any way with anyone, I wonder, why was I even born?

People talk all the time about having some purpose, some God-given reason for being alive. On TV shows like *I Survived*, people who had close encounters of the scariest kind, horrible near-death events, often say, "It just wasn't my time to die," or "God has plans for me."

So what is God's big plan for me? Why am I alive if no one can ever know me? There are about seven billion of us on the planet now. We are eating, pooping, arguing, sleeping, waking up, robbing banks, dressing little kids to send them off to school, reading, watching TV, blowing up things, praying, laughing, planning murders, planning families, passing the sugar or pulling the trigger on a shotgun—how do I fit into all of this?

After what happened with my dad, I have felt this need to make a connection with someone. And that's part of the reason—other than her pure, utter *hotness*—that my crush on Ally overwhelmed me. I wanted to find some way to know her and be known by her. My dreams helped me pretend that I was in love with someone and being loved in return. Without that ever happening for real, what does my life mean to anyone? To Mom? Dad? Paul and Cindy? Ally? Heck, I don't even know what my life means to me now. . . .

. . . but all my deep philosophical thoughts are interrupted . . .

. . . by a low growl. . . .

Okay, God, answer me this one, what does my life mean to Rusty with his huge fangs and wolf's eyes? And don't tell me that it means he'd love to eat me for dinner—I'm scared enough of him already!

12

Cindy and Ally are hanging out in the family room. Paul and his best friend, Tim Gunther, come through the front door, joking around about something. Paul spins a basketball really fast on the tip of his finger. I'd love to be able to do cool stuff like spinning a ball or juggling. I think jugglers look super cool handling three, four, maybe even five or more flying objects, one hand to the other, and the risky things like flaming torches, knives, and chain saws are even more awesome. I'd also love to learn how to put my fingers in my mouth and whistle loud enough to blow out your eardrums. You see, when you can't do anything, you have lots of time to think about all the stuff you wish you could do.

Walking into the kitchen, Tim notices Cindy and Ally first. He seems to blush a little as he says, "Hey."

Paul looks away from his spinning basketball, tosses it into the air off the tip of his finger, grabs it, and says, "Hi."

Ally smiles and says hi back. Cindy doesn't say anything.

Paul asks, "Whatcha doin'?"

Cindy says, "We were gonna watch a movie."

Paul asks, "Oh yeah, which one?"

The storage area of the cabinet on which our big-screen TV sits houses hundreds of flicks.

Ally answers, "We're thinkin' maybe *Rain Man*."

Paul laughs. "I'm an excellent driver," he says, imitating and quoting a line from the character Raymond, the autistic man in the movie who is every bit as addicted to driving his dad's 1958 Buick Roadmaster as Debi is to saying, "I like McDonnos."

Cindy and Ally laugh at Paul's excellent mimicry of obsessive Raymond. *Rain Man* is a favorite around here; we have lots of movies about messed-up heroes. Although *Rain Man* is probably number one on our disability hit parade, there are plenty of others. Most are about brain-damaged types: *My Left Foot*, *I Am Sam*, *Riding the Bus with My Sister*, *To Kill a Mockingbird* ("Hey, Boo Radley"), *Regarding Henry*, and even the much maligned *Tropic Thunder* ("You went full retard, you never wanna go full retard"). I personally believe that Mom wants to educate the world, one DVD viewing at a time, about people like me and now people like Debi too.

As I watch from my spot across the family room, I see something I've never noticed before: Cindy and Tim are an item too. They keep trying not to stare at each other, but they can't stop themselves. Every time they make eye contact, they both blush and quickly look away, only to come back to gazing into each other's eyes a few seconds later. Paul and Ally do this whole gazing thing too. But, like I said before, they act like they've been together forever. I don't know for how long Cindy and Tim have felt this way about each other, but it's clear to me that they want to keep it a secret.

Ally asks the guys, "You want to watch with us?"

Paul says, "Nah, we're gonna shoot some hoops—" He pauses and asks, "Sorry, Timbo, do you wanna watch *Rain Man*?"

Tim hesitates a moment before he answers, "I've never seen it."

"Really?" Paul says. "My mom would shoot you! If you'd rather watch, we can—it's a great movie."

Tim asks, "You sure?"

"For sure," Paul says. Now imitating Raymond's flat, emotionless, weird way of speaking again, he says, "Qantas . . . Qantas has never crashed."

"What?" Tim asks.

Paul laughs. "You'll see."

Cindy spins my wheelchair so that I can see the TV

too. They move to the kitchen and grab some snacks, and Paul slips me a bite of potato chip and pours a sip of Coke into my mouth. Most of this food and drink dribbles down my chin. I'm glad that Rusty is in the backyard—otherwise he might eat my head. What dog could resist the temptation to chow down on a potato-chip, Coke-soaked snack of retard face? Sheesh, for a guy who wanted to juggle chain saws five minutes ago, I sure can turn into a wimp fast.

Minutes later we're all watching Dustin Hoffman and Tom Cruise play two adult brothers. Tom Cruise is Charlie Babbitt, a selfish, impatient businessman forced into taking care of his older autistic brother, Raymond, whom he hardly knows. Raymond has an amazing memory like mine, but his thing is for baseball and numbers. As the story unfolds, Charlie learns to love and admire his disabled brother. The movie is kind of like Paul's and my relationship. Except of course that Paul has no idea I'm smart and he never will.

Speaking of Paul, he's sitting on the couch, his arm draped comfortably over Ally's shoulder. Her right hand rests on top of his leg.

Tim sits on the floor next to Cindy. They are a little way apart and they aren't letting Paul or Ally notice that every so often they sneak their hands along the floor until they touch. Once touching, they grasp hands briefly, their fingers rubbing together, then quickly pull away so they won't get caught.

Why they are trying to hide this, I don't know. Maybe this is a requirement of Tim and Paul's friendship, or maybe Cindy is embarrassed that Paul will find out. But I can't stop thinking, selfishly, full of self-pity, that Ally has Paul and he has her. It's good seeing Cindy and Tim like this. But before, I felt like part of the group, and now I'm just the fifth wheel. Who do I have? Who will I ever have? I zone out of the movie and wonder if I can survive—being alone and feeling so lonely. Again I ask myself, "Was Dad right to want to kill me? Would it be better to be out of my misery?"

Okay, shake it off, Prince Pity Party! Enough is enough already!

It's just the way it is. . . .

Think about better stuff. . . .

Get a grip!

13

As if suffering through the *Rain Man* lovefest yesterday wasn't enough, today is my birthday. Yaaaaaay!

It's hard to lose the sarcasm. How can I get juiced about birthdays anymore? Today I'm fifteen years old, and I'm pretty sure this birthday is going to be exactly like birthdays fourteen and thirteen and twelve and . . . you get the picture.

My day started with Paul singing me his version of the Beatles's *White Album* song "Birthday." We've always been a Beatles-addicted family—I know all the words to all their songs. Paul's rendition, screeching the violent-sounding guitar solos, is grating and annoying in a hilarious way. And it's not as if Paul can help himself. He sings this song to everyone in the house on their birthday and to all his friends over the phone on their birthday, as well. And he *really* rocks it, 'til your ears are ringing, if not bleeding, but you almost don't mind.

My mom brought to my school earlier today a white cake with white frosting that had red and blue and green and pink frosted balloons on it and the words "Happy Birthday, Shawn." My Diaper-Changer William and Gorgeous-Steaming-Hot Becky, the teacher's aides, and Mrs. Hare, the teacher, and my classmates gathered around my chair and sang "Happy Birthday." Well, I should say that a few of the kids sang—those who wanted to and could actually sing. The rest of us just sort of sat there like we always do, lumps of mostly silent humanoid non-playas.

After the song I was, of course, unable to blow out any candles. But somehow, all the kids, led by several who tend to salivate and spit a lot when they "help," managed to extinguish them and make my birthday wish come true— which was for the candles to go out before the smoke alarm went off.

As if we didn't look bad enough already, we all got ugly, pointy birthday party hats attached to our skulls (Debi would have loved them). Next we had the cake.

The kids who could eat on their own scarfed down their pieces of cake and then signaled or asked for more. The kids who couldn't feed themselves, like me, got bites spooned into their mouths. When we were finished, it looked like a cake explosion had taken place. Frosting and mashed cake covered everyone's faces, chins, eyebrows, and pointy-hat tips. Cake on our bibs and hands and pant legs. Cake and frosting smeared into chairs and on the floor underneath. Really, it's amazing how one little cake can spread so far when being fed to me and my special needs classmates.

Tonight, at my family party, the big surprise is when my dad shows up. This is the first time Dad's been back here since that night he tried to . . . you know. I gotta admit it feels pretty weird. As he walks into the house, he hands Mom a birthday card for me, no doubt including a check for the occasion, and Mom says, "Thanks."

Dad hugs Cindy, waves to Debi rather uncomfortably, and then holds out his hand to Paul, who shakes it. To say Paul and Dad have had a rocky relationship is putting it mildly. Paul has never been able to forgive Dad for bailing on us after I was born so messed up. But recently things have been better. Now Paul is civil to Dad and will speak to him.

Dad says to Paul, "Your mom says you are homing in on a school—maybe Stanford or U-dub."

Paul looks at Dad, takes a quick breath, and says, "Yeah. Nothing's for sure yet."

"Well," Dad says, "whatever you decide, we're with you."

I can see the wheels turning in Paul's head, almost hear

him self-censoring all kinds of smart-ass things he would say if their uneasy cease-fire weren't in place.

Finally Paul smiles. "Thanks, but we're here for Big Boy's fifteenth, right?"

Dad smiles too. "Absolutely," he says, adding, *"Quince-añero."*

It's fine with me if they use me to avoid their conflict. I mean, think about it, it's really the only way I've ever been able to help my brother—well, other than letting him steal my girlfriend who didn't know she was my girlfriend, but I digress.

Debi is sulking and mumbling and looking pissed because she hasn't been able to stick with her routine tonight.

Paul tries to cheer her up. "You look nice today, Debi," he says.

Debi smiles at Paul and says, "I like when you say dat."

Cindy catches the vibe and, maybe trying to add on to the Debi-looks-nice theme, asks Debi if she has a boyfriend. Debi smiles even wider. "Dat's for me to know and you to find out." She laughs at her joke.

Mom insists that Debi join us for my birthday party, which, now that dinner is done, consists of having yet another birthday cake, after which I'll "open" my presents. I already know that these so-called presents will be the usuals: socks, T-shirts, and bib overalls with snaps on the inseams so I can have my diaper changed easily. In other words, my birthday presents are just normal things that I need anyway, wrapped in brightly colored kiddy wrapping paper that my family "helps me" tear off.

"I like presents!" Debi says, eyeing my gifts.

"Yes," Mom says, "presents are fun. These are for Shawn's birthday."

Debi looks bummed. She glances away from the presents and mumbles, "I like McDonnos."

Dad asks, "What?"

Everyone else just ignores it.

"Happy birf-day, S-S-S-Swan," Debi says, breaking the awkward silence.

I think, "Tanks a million Deb-o-reeno!"

When Debi spots the cake, chocolate this time, and the tub of French vanilla ice cream, her spirits seem to rise dramatically.

Everybody sings "Happy Birthday" to me and Mom cuts the cake, scoops on the ice cream, and serves each of us.

She feeds me a bite at a time, while everyone else eats too. My eyes drift to the faces around the table, everyone smiles and visits with one another, even Debi seems happy. I understand that birthdays are the one day out of a year when a person should get to feel special just for being alive.

On my birthdays I have always wondered why I was

born. My parents divorced because of me. My Mom lugs me around like an overgrown baby all day. And nobody thinks that I'm anything more than a guy with the mental abilities of large zucchini squash and a broken drool switch stuck on high. But I look at these faces again, my family and Debi, and they all look so happy, truly happy to be here celebrating me.

Why can't I just be happy too? Seriously, what the hell's gotten into me lately? Okay, Shawn, that's it! I mean it! Be honest. This year doesn't feel as much like a farce. Dad showed up. I'm still alive. I've had two cakes in one day. My family cares about me enough to be happy that I was born, glad that I'm here with them. Plus I have new socks. I *really* like new socks!

Is this your life, Shawn?

Yer damned straight it is!

Cheer up!

Get a flippin' clue, dude!

Some things never change . . . then again some things *do!*

14

Yes, things are changing. Debi and Rusty have been living here for three weeks. Rusty hasn't eaten me, and life with them has started to feel . . . normal?

"Normal" isn't right, because I don't think it's possible to have a "normal" life with me in the house. At least not like the homes of families I see on TV. But weird as we might be, Debi and Rusty coming here has juiced up our lives. They have changed us, and we're living a new definition of "normal."

Debi has a routine: She gets up every morning, Monday through Friday, makes her bed, and makes her own lunch for school. Debi is a stickler for putting her laundry away. Mom says that Debi's bedroom is by far the tidiest spot in the house.

Each morning Debi unloads the dishwasher without

being asked. Unfortunately, a couple days ago, Mom hadn't run the dishwasher the night before, so the dishes were still dirty; Debi put them away anyway. After her chores, she sits on the little bench in the entryway and waits for her white, square paratransit bus to take her to "schoo." The same bus brings her back home at around four. To be honest, I'm glad I don't have to take that bus. It doesn't look to me anything like a high-end limo service.

On weekends Debi hangs out in the basement and plays her favorite movie over and over and over again. She calls this movie *The Sound of* the *Music* and she's watched it, and this is not an exaggeration, two times each Saturday and two more times each Sunday every weekend since she moved in. And she plays it LOUD! My main sitting spot upstairs is right above a heat vent that carries the sound. So I've heard "Doe, a deer, a female deer; ray, a drop of golden sun" and every other line from every other song twelve times over the last three weeks. I have no reason to believe I won't hear it another four times every weekend for the rest of our lives together. One word: torture.

Yesterday when Debi returned from school, Mom noticed something odd in her appearance. "Debi," Mom asked, "are you hiding something under your coat?"

Debi said, "No hiding . . . it okay."

Mom approached her and said, "I need to see what you have, honey." Mom gently pulled Debi's coat open.

Stuffed into the arms of the coat and under her shirt, down the front of her pants, and even into her bra, were plastic bags. Mom helped her pull them out, counting as she went: twenty-eight, ranging from the small, light-weight bags they give you at supermarkets to carry your apples to the larger ones you get when they ask "Will that be paper or plastic?" Apparently Debi is the unofficial plastic bag collector for the North Neighborhood Community Center.

"What are all these for?" Mom asked Debi.

Debi didn't answer right away. "I need dem."

Mom asked, "What for?"

Debi said, "To go with me . . . my bed."

"Your bed?" Mom asked.

"Under," Debi answered.

Mom followed Debi downstairs and twenty minutes later came back upstairs carrying a huge armful of plastic bags, hundreds and hundreds of them, some covered in dust bunnies and all of them mashed together, wrinkled up into a giant ball. Debi must have been bringing them home every day.

Cindy said sarcastically, "Well, everybody needs a hobby."

Mom gave Cindy a dirty look, but Debi said, "Yeth, hoppy good," and laughed.

Mom said, "There isn't enough space in your bedroom,

Debi, for so many of these bags. We'll have to get rid of a few."

Debi kind of nodded and mostly just stared at the floor.

But the plastic bag collection wasn't all Mom found. While pulling out the bags, Mom also discovered twenty-three library books, ranging from kids' picture books to three volumes, A, B, and D, of the *World Book* encyclopedia.

Mom asked, "Do you have a library card?"

Debi answered, "It okay . . . don't need."

Debi somehow managed to steal all these books, getting them through the book detector machines at the downtown public library during field trips there with her Learning Skills group.

Mom said, "Actually, Debi, you need to check books out when you borrow them from the library."

Debi said, "No, they free."

Mom said, "They're free to *borrow*, Debi."

Debi answered, "No borrow . . . keep 'em . . . I like 'em."

Mom sighed and said, "No, Debi, we have to return these."

"Dat okay," Debi said. "Dey got more."

I'm not sure Mom's efforts to explain to Debi the concept of a lending library made a lot of sense to Debi, but in the end she said, "It okay, Linny . . . I okay."

Like I said, our family is making a new normal because of Debi.

And Rusty is part of this too. Rusty has become the family dog. Well, more truthfully, Paul's dog, although Debi doesn't seem to mind or notice. Rusty and Paul wrestle all over the house with Rusty barking and wagging his tail, jumping and scratching and biting Paul in ways that leave little red streaks on his arms and hands but never break the skin. Paul gives as good as he gets, tossing Rusty off him and slapping him around in ways that make Rusty more and more excited and playful.

Paul has Rusty trained really well. They can be fighting, rolling around, looking like they might kill each other, and then Paul just says, "Rusty, sit," with a certain tone in his voice. Immediately, Rusty will plant his butt on the floor. If Paul commands, "Stay," he can walk away and Rusty won't budge. When Paul says, "Okay," Rusty will come running back up to him, wagging his tail.

Paul has even trained Rusty not to attack and bite the wheels of my wheelchair anymore. From his very first day here, the dog has thought of my wheelchair as a dangerous satanic object that requires constant monitoring and attention. Despite Paul's training, whenever Rusty comes into a room where I am, he dips his head low, staring with scary intensity at my beautiful chrome ride; sometimes the fur on his neck puffs up and he lets out a low growl. I wish I could explain to him, "Hey Rusty, I don't like this wheelchair any more than you do."

Actually, I'm still scared of Rusty. Even though he's average size—I heard Cindy say fifty-five pounds—he's so strong and powerful. If he wanted to hurt me, he could do it easily. So far he hasn't mistaken my leg as part of the evil enemy wheelchair—so far.

15

Debi came home from "schoo" yesterday and announced to Mom, "I no friends with B-B-B-Barbara no more."

Mom said, "Did something happen at school today?"

"Yeth," Debi answered.

Mom asked, "Did you and Barbara quarrel?"

"No me," Debi answered, "J-J-J-Janeth."

"Janet and Barbara quarreled?"

"Yeth . . . no quarry . . . hit and bite."

Mom asked, "But you didn't hit or get involved?"

"No tanks," Debi answered.

Mom said, "Well that's good, sweetie. You just be nice to everyone and they'll be nice to you, right?"

"Yeth," Debi answered, but I'm not sure she really

accepted Mom's logic. Truthfully, I'm never sure how much Debi gets or doesn't get out of any conversation.

Thinking about Debi, I wonder about her seeing her two classmates hit and bite each other. No matter what advice Mom gives her, Debi is pretty much defenseless. If you think about that word, it's pretty heavy. *Defenseless.* It never means "less defense." It means *no* defense. When a person is defenseless, it means that he can't defend himself at all, right?

Sometimes I get scared that I'm defenseless, too. Debi is slow, but at least she can run away or yell or hit back if someone is bothering her. When you look at me, you'd think I am completely defenseless. And technically my only defenses are my central nervous system, the automatic part of my brain—the kind of defenses no one ever thinks about. If I never blinked, my eyes would quickly dry out and I'd become blind, but my eyes blink when they need to; if something like a fly or a gnat gets near them, my eyelids do their job. I also breathe, sleep, awaken, swallow, wiggle, shift positions, stretch, yawn, laugh, excrete, and dream. In these supersimple ways, my body takes care of itself. Also, it's not like I'm paralyzed; I feel sensations of touch like pain and pleasure and I react to these feelings. When the doctor hits my knee with his little rubber hammer, my lower leg kicks. If you grab me by my arm and squeeze too tight, I'll cry out. I can't will my body to do what I say, but my body wills me to do what it says.

We consider old people and babies as being defenseless, but if you think about it, most everyone in the world can easily become defenseless. Swim in the ocean and get eaten by a great white shark. Jump from an airplane 150 times for fun, and on the 151st jump, your parachute and your backup chute both fail. While walking into your house from the mailbox on a cloudy day, you get struck by a bolt of lightning. If you think of it that way, we're all always at risk at some time or another. And either by chance or bad luck or even by just living long enough to get old and weak, every one of us ends up defenseless. It just so happens I'm like this all the time.

As I sit in the family room by my window, my head happens to shift and Rusty comes into focus. He's lying on the floor in what has become the regular spot for him, the passage between the family room and the kitchen, where Mom is cleaning up. I see Debi in the background, out of focus, waiting for her bus. Paul and Cindy have already taken off for school.

Rusty stares at me and I look back at him. He doesn't growl now, but he doesn't blink or look away either. We gaze straight into each other's eyes.

It occurs to me that Rusty is definitely *not* defenseless.

This thought, however, is immediately crushed by another more pressing realization—I'm slipping into a seizure.

16

A slow, low buzz starts to hum inside my head and I know instantly what it is: the weird zone before my seizure gets a full grip on me. In these last few seconds before my spirit escapes, I see my mom. She hasn't noticed that my seizure has started, so instead of coming to my side to comfort me, she turns and leaves the kitchen, walking up the stairs toward her room.

Debi's bus arrives.

I hear Mom say, "Have fun at school, Debi."

Debi calls, "B-b-b-bye," and goes out the door.

I'm just about to slip away from my body when I focus on Rusty. He was calm and quiet a few moments ago, but now the fur on the back of his neck rises as he watches me. I twitch around, drool even more heavily than usual, and am unable to breathe for several long seconds.

Rusty starts to inch toward me, growls low, and bares his teeth. I can't blame him for being scared—even normal human beings get frightened watching me have a grand mal seizure, but people know better than to attack me. I don't know what Rusty is going to do.

As I've said, I love my seizures and my chance to escape my body for a while. But although I can usually will myself to stick around, in this seizure I can't. My spirit leaves my body and flies far away before I can see what Rusty will do next.

I find myself in a library with a large glass wall, looking over a river raging down below. *Where is this place?* I am sitting in a comfortable chair—I can feel my butt on the soft cushions of the upholstered seat, and I lean against its upholstered back, eyeing the rows of shelves holding thousands of books.

Suddenly, from the corner of my eye, I see a dark figure move quickly behind one of the bookshelves. *Who is it? What is it?* I don't know how I know, but I sense that this figure has been staring at me.

I want to go look, but now I feel too hot, like I'm being suffocated under a stack of pillows. I feel like I am gasping, struggling to get enough oxygen. *What is going on here?*

* * *

I awaken from the seizure, slowly coming back to my senses. I'm confused and a little frightened. I've never had a dream like this before. My dreams and seizures usually feel the same to me, but this one feels more like a nightmare than a dream. Who was that dark figure? What did it want with me? A chill runs through my body, a shiver of fear. After a few moments, I realize that I'm still in my wheelchair, my head tilted way back, staring at the ceiling. My breaths come in short, panting gasps. Finally my head drops forward so that I'm looking out the window, seeing my regular view of the water. But I still feel suffocated, and only now do I realize why I'm so hot; Rusty has hoisted his front paws onto my legs and has draped himself over my body. Although he seems calm, his head is raised, his expression attentive and alert, totally in control. Rusty has felt my fear and he has overcome his own fear of my wheelchair. He is protecting me. Somehow, in his dog brain, Rusty understands that I am *not* my wheelchair, I am alive and here with him.

I can't make myself look at him, but after a few moments, he seems to sense that I've noticed him lying across my lap. I'd like to say, "Good dog, Rusty, you can get off me. I'm okay." Of course I can't say this, but as I'm thinking it, Rusty shifts his head, arching his neck so that he gazes directly into my eyes. He makes a tiny whine, as if he's saying something back to me, and gently lifts himself up and drops to the floor.

My head shifts and I'm looking at Rusty again as he goes back to his favorite spot and lies down. He looks back at me, lowers his head onto his front paws, and stares, as if he is waiting to see if I might need him again. I think, "I'm okay now, Rusty—you can relax." Rusty cocks his head as if he's unsure, watches me for a moment, and seems satisfied as he rolls onto his side, takes a deep breath, and slides into a nap.

Rusty defended me. He is my friend. A new feeling rises up inside me and overwhelms me—*I have a friend!* And I know that he feels it too. I now realize that I have nothing, nada, zilch, zippo, zero to fear from him.

By adding this moment to my birthday realization, that I have more to be happy about than my pouty, crybaby attitude has been letting me see, I realize that there're a few more pretty cool things about being *me*!

1. I've finally made a connection with another living soul. Unfortunately, that soul didn't belong to another human being, but hey, it belongs to a dog! And Rusty, my protector and friend, doesn't give a rip what I look like or act like—what I can and can't do—Rusty's a *real* friend!
2. Obviously, it feels good that Dad did not decide to kill me. Imagine how Dad would feel if he

somehow knew that Rusty and I had found a way to connect. I mean, I'm sure part of Dad's thoughts about ending my pain must have been tied to my loneliness. And with Rusty here I'm not alone anymore!

You might ask, how can you turn a self-pity party into a positive? My answer is simple: Just pay attention to your world.

3. Cindy just played my favorite Mozart (Sonata for Piano in D, adagio movement).
4. A few minutes ago, I heard Mom laugh on the phone, her loud, happy, totally real laugh, which reminded me that she's the coolest mom in the world.
5. Yesterday I saw two sparrows mating out on the railing of our deck—hey, gimme a break, a guy's gotta get his jollies when he can.
6. A ton of self-pity lifts off my shoulders like a cloud of morning fog evaporating in the sunlight. A flood of thoughts races through my mind about how my life is great: the view from my window of Puget Sound, my sister's sweet smile, Mom's patience when she feeds me. And now about a billion more ridiculously random good things:

Corvette automobiles, cool T-shirts, the wail of a sad saxophone, pralines 'n cream ice cream, soft breezes, and the way totally new socks feel when Mom first slips them onto my feet.

7. Thanks to Rusty, I can seriously jump-start my life and drop all this "poor-me" crap. There're way too many things to enjoy.

17

Since I've been in special education classrooms for all my life, I've spent a lot of time around developmentally disabled people, including kids with Down. But I've never understood any of them the way I do now, living full-time with the Debster. She's an adult like Mom but she's stuck mentally with a young child's mind.

Debi doesn't require a lot of attention. She doesn't like to watch TV with the family or interact with us very much. She prefers to follow her own very rigid schedule: making her lunch in the morning, going to school, eating dinner as soon as she gets home at 4 p.m., then a shower and quiet time in her room. Whenever Mom invites her to join us, she always gets the same answer, "Shower now . . . bed . . . I tired."

But I gotta admit, things are not always sugar and spice

and everything nice with Debi. She has bad moods that sometimes last for an entire evening and stretch into the next morning.

Like yesterday. Debi brought home a flier for Summer Funshine Bible Camp for Special Needs Adults and demanded that Mom sign her up. Mom had asked, "Are you sure you want to go to this?"

"Yeth," Debi said firmly. "My course is yeth . . . my choice."

Mom said, "Of course it's your choice, Debi, and if you'd like to go—"

Debi interrupted, sounding almost angry, "I say YETH! I want go, YETH!"

"Okay, Debi," Mom answered, "I'll sign you up."

Her mission accomplished, Debi turned and stomped out of the room, hunched over and looking angry.

This morning Debi walks into the kitchen just as grumpy as she was yesterday. "Can I say some'tin?"

Mom looks at Debi and kind of smiles. "Of course, Debi."

Debi says, "No Bible camp!"

Mom asks, "You don't want to go to Bible camp after all?"

"No," Debi says.

Mom asks, "You've changed your mind?"

Debi just stares at her.

Mom says, "Debi, you have decided you don't want to go to Bible camp after all?"

Debi still stares, her expression confused and unhappy. Finally she says, "No go!"

Mom says, "Okay, I'll cancel your registration."

Debi just stands there looking pissed off.

I know that my mood has been pretty rotten lately too, but I wonder what has gotten Debi all worked up. I know the frustration of having something eating away at you and not being able to express yourself.

But you can turn your outlook around if you want to badly enough. Knowing that Rusty is watching out for me really lifts my spirits—and even though I can't have Ally, I'm glad that she has a good guy like Paul, and proud that my brother landed such a hottie. And Cindy came home holding hands with Tim last night—you shoulda seen her face, I couldn't help but feel happy for her. Maybe Debi will pick up on this vibe too and catch a ride on the love train.

18

"*WHAT THE BLEEP . . . ?*" Mom is screaming, and my mom *never* screams. And *bleep* is a swear word I've *never* heard her say before.

Both Paul and Cindy jump up.

"What is it?" Paul yells. I feel his adrenaline from ten feet away.

Mom screams, "MY God . . . *NO*," this time more sad than angry. And now I hear her sob.

Cindy cries, "Mom!"

Mom says, "My albums . . . my God . . . NO! They're ruined! They're—" Her sobs cut her words off as Paul and Cindy reach her side. Mom's been putting together family albums, histories made up of pictures and press clippings, school photos and miscellaneous stuff. I know how important these albums are to Mom because she's often asked

Cindy or Paul to stay with me so that she can go to the Scrapbook Store and have old pictures blown up and reprinted.

Mom, standing stiff and clenching and unclenching her fists, cries "DEBI!" at the top of her voice. I can see Mom trying to calm down and getting control of herself as she marches downstairs. We can all hear her speaking to Debi, loudly and firmly, without any threats or violence, but making it *very* clear that Mom's scrapbook albums are one hundred percent *off*-limits from now on.

It takes me a while to get the whole story straight. At her day program, Debi cuts up magazines and makes collages from the pictures. She does this each week on crafts day. Every Wednesday, when Debi gets home, she proudly displays her day's efforts. Her collages are cutout pictures of car ads and shampoo models, miscellaneous food items: pizza, a bag of frozen peas, and a hot dog on a plate. Sometimes she's included a speedboat or a racecar and anything relating to Disneyland or Winnie the Pooh. These are often in weird combinations: a newspaper shot of some mother on trial for killing her own child right next to a picture of a kitten with a ball of string. A blurry image from a surveillance camera of a suspect in a 7-Eleven holdup and a dinner plate piled high with carrots. You can never tell what might make its way into one of Debi's creations or why it's there.

Apparently Debi discovered Mom's scrapbooks and

grabbed her scissors and glue stick and made what I'm sure she felt were big improvements: cutting off the top of Cindy's head from her fourth-grade school picture; removing Paul's legs from a newspaper photo of him running with a football; cutting me altogether from quite a few family shots.

Talk about your perfect setup for a big-boom disaster—Mom's albums and Debi's "art." Mom always makes a big deal of Debi's collages because she knows that to Debi they are important, but Debi had no clue about the difference in value between Mom's precious albums and Debi's chopped-up-magazine art. I don't think there was anything especially logical about Debi's choices of who to cut, and I'm sure that nothing she did was meant to be hurtful. Everyone thinks I'm a veg. But I'm smart. I know right from wrong, whether anybody knows this about me or not. They think that I can't be bad or mean or hurtful. That's not really true. I do get irritated like when Debi makes me crazy watching *The Sound of the Music* over and over again at supersonic sound. And you already know about my sarcasm. In this situation with Mom and Debi, I feel I'm connecting in other ways. I can feel other people's heartbreak and pain and grief. I feel sorry for Debi that she's in trouble for something she didn't know was wrong, and I feel sad for my mom for what's she's lost.

* * *

After Mom comes back upstairs from scolding Debi, I hear her talking to Paul and Cindy in the family room.

Mom says, "A university in central Missouri is collecting all your father's papers."

"Papers?" Paul asks.

Mom explains. "Anything to do with his career as a poet and writer."

Cindy asks, "The family albums were for them?"

"Not now," Mom explains, "and for as long as either of you want to keep any family things, of course they're yours. But Shawn isn't ever going to have a family, be a father, or have children. And since your dad's career is so closely attached to Shawn's life, it felt good to me, comforting to know that Shawn would live on, that his album would be of interest to people years and years from now, after we're all gone. But now it's ruined—your brother's album, irreplaceable photographs of Shawn as a baby . . . all the—" She starts crying again.

Tears are weird things for me; sometimes they show up without my even feeling sad, other times the most heartbreaking news in the world—stuff that makes me wish I could scream and weep and beat up the whole universe— leaves me dry-eyed. But hearing Mom talk about her album she made for me, how making it somehow made my condition and my life easier for her to handle and helped her feel better—well, to be honest, that made me feel worse. I have a sick, empty, gnarly feeling in the pit of my stomach. I wish I could cry right now.

An hour or so later, after Mom has calmed down and Cindy and Paul have gone up to their rooms, I can see Mom in the kitchen and overhear her on the phone, telling my dad what has happened. I can tell that Dad is reassuring her. She nods sometimes, a funny habit she has when she's talking on the phone, as if the person on the other end of the line can see her.

"I know," Mom says finally. "Thanks for talking me down." She pauses, laughs a little, and says, "No, really, I feel better. I'm not even sure how many photos are wrecked—I didn't have the heart to look all through."

She is quiet again. "I know," she says, "you too. . . . Thanks and good night." Mom hangs up the phone.

Rusty lies at her feet and stares up at her. She looks down at him. "You're not in any trouble, Mr. Rustoleum," she says. "Catastrophe canceled. Everything's going to be okay now. I'm sure Debi has learned her lesson."

19

The next morning, Debi's bus picks her up for "schoo" and Mom is getting ready to take me to my schoo . . . I mean my school.

The doorbell chimes. Rusty barks like a maniac until Mom shushes him and says, "Lie down," which he does as she answers the front door.

I can't tell who's here until Mom walks into the kitchen, followed by a uniformed officer of the Seattle Police Department. He's a young-looking guy, in his early twenties, and even though my mom looks pretty much like your typical suburban housewife, this young cop actually has his hand resting on the handle of his gun. His eyes shift back and forth across the room, like he's expecting to be attacked at any second.

Mom says, "You're welcome to look around."

"Thank you, ma'am," the cop says in a stern no-nonsense voice. He adds, "We take emergency calls very seriously."

Mom says, "Yes, of course."

Emergency calls? What's going on? Lately, Paul hasn't been raging around as much, but did something make my brother lose his temper and go off on somebody again, the way he used to? Is Cindy okay? Maybe something is up with Dad?

Mom says, "I'm so sorry about this."

But the cop ignores her and asks, "May I go downstairs?"

"Of course," Mom says. She pauses. Then she adds, "Debi left about ten minutes ago and should be at the North Neighborhood Community Center soon. You can go there and see for yourself that she's okay."

Debi? What the hell?

I hear them moving around downstairs, and in spite of Rusty's whining I can still get most of what Mom is saying.

"Yes," Mom says, "she lost her father a little over two months ago and has been with us . . . the change has probably been very traumatic . . . must have used the phone in the laundry room . . . I scolded her last night . . . ruining my albums . . ."

Now I hear the cop: "We have to respond to any . . ."

Mom again. "Of course . . . I'll talk to her . . . I'm sure that . . ."

Now they have disappeared deeper into the basement, probably into Debi's room because I can't hear them at all.

Soon they come back upstairs to where I'm sitting and the policeman, who looks far more relaxed, says, "It's good that she knows how to use 911, but she needs to understand that it's for emergencies only."

Mom says, "Of course. I'll talk with her about this when she gets home. I'll make sure she understands."

The cop nods at Mom. "Everything here looks fine."

I'm thinking, "Hey officer, if I could speak, I'd tell you all about Debi. Sometimes she has her moods, but she's also funny and goofy, like her red cowboy hat that first morning, like her joking around with Cindy and Paul. She doesn't do bad things from meanness. In fact, most of the time she doesn't seem to have a clue what's really going on." Instead what comes from my mouth is "Ahhhhhhh."

He glances at me.

Mom says, "My son Shawn."

The cop smiles. "I've got a son too."

Mom says, "Really? You look so young."

The cop blushes. "Well, he's only eighteen months."

The police officer looks toward me and says, "Hi there."

When I don't say anything back, Mom says, "Shawn's profoundly disabled. He's not being rude—he can't understand or speak."

The cop nods and looks at the floor. He takes a quick

breath. "You've got quite a handful here, ma'am."

Mom forces a smile.

The policeman says, "If you ever have any problem at all, please don't hesitate to call us, okay?"

"I won't, officer."

They are walking toward the front door when Mom adds, "If you need to check in later, feel free."

The cop says, "That won't be necessary, ma'am. I appreciate your cooperation and I'm sorry to have interrupted your day. Thank you."

Mom says, "Thank you."

The cop doesn't say anything more until they get to the door. "You take care."

"We will," Mom says. A couple moments later, his car door slams and his engine starts.

Mom watches as the police officer drives away. She turns to Rusty and says, "Shall we dig up Debi's body from the garden now?" She laughs. "I know, not very funny, but can you imagine that little pill calling 911 because I scolded her?"

Rusty stares at Mom intently. "And a better question," Mom says, shaking her head, "is why am I talking to a dog?"

Rusty glances at me, and I wonder if he's thinking, "You talk to Shawn all the time too, and he never answers!"

20

When Debi gets home, Mom welcomes her like she does every day.

"Hi, Debi," Mom says.

"Hi," Debi says, as happy and cheerful as can be.

Mom lets her set down her lunch box, her purse, and her backpack.

Debi comes into the kitchen.

Mom says, "Debi, you called 911 this morning, didn't you?"

Debi doesn't say anything, just stops dead in her tracks and stares at the floor.

"Debi," Mom says again.

Still silence.

Mom, "You need to answer my question, Debi. I'm not

mad at you, but we need to talk about this. You called 911 this morning, didn't you?"

Debi stares at the floor for what seems like about a hundred years. Finally she speaks so low I can barely hear her. "Yeth, Linny."

Mom asks, "Were you afraid you were in trouble for cutting up my family albums?"

Debi says, "I sorry."

Mom says, "It's all right—we love you, but you can't call 911 unless there is a real emergency, do you understand?"

"I sorry," Debi says.

"Were you afraid, Debi?"

"Mad. . . . I sorry."

"You were angry?"

"I like McDonnos."

Mom smiles. "I know you do, Debi, and we'll go there for lunch on Saturday if you promise no more 911 calls unless the house is on fire, okay?"

"Yeth," Debi says.

Now Mom says, "You can't call 911 every time you get angry."

Debi nods and says, "I sorry."

Mom gives her a hug, and as they are hugging, Debi asks, "Can I say some'tin?"

"Of course, sweetie," Mom says.

I think to myself, this is Debi's eureka moment. She's going to own up right now, take responsibility, and apologize beyond her rote "I sorry" line. She'll show that she understands what happened and why Mom was so upset. She'll apologize!

Debi hesitates, but finally she speaks. "What's for dinner?" she asks, as if the whole previous conversation never even occurred.

Without missing a beat, Mom answers, "How about some homemade split-pea soup?"

"Dat sounds good," Debi answers.

But this is what she says *every* afternoon when she gets home. It's part of her ritual. Every day she asks "What's for dinner?" and I'm convinced Mom could say, "Spoiled, sour-owl poop and a bed of rotting maggot-covered e-coli spinach," and Debi would respond with "Dat sounds good."

But who am I to poke fun at Debi? She can't rise above her limitations. And how is that any different from anybody else? Everyone has limits and blind spots. Being human means having a mix of both strengths and weaknesses. I think the majority of people who see Debi and me focus on our weaknesses and are oblivious to our strengths. I know I've been ragging on Debi, but she always tells the truth, or at least tries to, and she's got a great sense of humor. Plus she never acts out of cruelty.

I, of all people, know what it feels like to be misunderstood. And I've got that whole weaknesses thing totally covered. But whether people see it or not, there are a few strengths lurking inside each of us too.

21

I'm in a wooded area, not really a big forest, just a small grove of evergreen trees, and the light dims, as if a dark cloud is passing before the sun.

I stretch out, my fists clench, my muscles tighten in my arms, my leg muscles flex too. Man, this feels incredibly great.

Looking into the trees, I catch just a glimpse—the tiniest, quick image—of a shadowy figure darting behind the thick wide trunk of an ancient pine. It's the same figure I saw when I was traveling in my earlier seizure, in that library by the raging river, when I woke up with Rusty in my lap.

This time I don't feel as scared as I did the last time, but I am curious. Why do I keep on dreaming about this dark figure? Who could it be, coming to watch me? Coming to spy on me and invade my dreams? Could it be someone

I know? I've never had any dreams or seizure travels like this before, where something so confusing keeps happening. What the hell is going on?

I call, "Hi."

I can't see the figure now. Why is it hiding from me?

I move toward the trees, and the closer I get, the more excited I feel.

Light streams down now, casting shadows through the branches. I look up and see the sun, bright, directly overhead, making splashes of light along the forest floor.

I reach the big tree and look behind it, anxious to see the figure. But no one is there, and again the sky darkens. Suddenly, I see the dark figure, far ahead, hurrying away, and this time it just evaporates, like molecules melting into thin air. A spirit? A ghost? Made of mist?

I awaken from this dream with sweat on my forehead and on the palms of my hands.

My dreams and spirit travels have always been the best part of my life. But now that I'm awake, I feel anxious. From the age of six I've always escaped my body, the trap that is my normal, waking life, through dreams and seizures. It's the only time I'm ever in control. Now, this strange, uninvited figure has ruined my great escape. I tell myself "don't be afraid," but even as I'm thinking this, goose bumps cover my body again, and a shiver runs through me. I *hate* my fear!

22

"Hi, s—s—s—Swan," Debi says, walking into the family room.

Of course I can't answer or acknowledge her.

She's quiet for a few moments, standing next to me.

My head shifts a little and I can see her staring through the window. Her light brown hair comes down almost to her shoulders. She's wearing a red T-shirt with something about a children's book festival on it, baggy gray pants, and black shoes with Velcro straps. She stands slightly stooped over, her mouth open a tiny bit. I can hear her breathing.

Several minutes pass. "Purtty," she says, still staring at the view.

I think back to her the words "Sorry, Debi, I don't do chitchat."

But she continues to just stand here, until finally she says, "I like McDonnos."

Great, I think, she's starting up her McDonald's mantra again. Does she think any of us are gonna forget that invaluable factoid about her? As I'm thinking this and trying not to feel annoyed, she speaks again, so softly that I can barely hear her, "I miss Mom and Dad." Her expression doesn't change. She just keeps staring out at the cold water, the cold world beyond our window.

A big lump forms in my throat. My skin tingles. I feel so sorry for her, and I realize McDonnos is not just a place for Debi. It's a fantasy where she can escape, at least for a few moments, her loneliness and loss. Of all the times I've wished I could speak, of all the words I've longed to say, I can't think of too many times when I wished it more than I wish it right now. But of course I can't speak. All I can do is think the words "I'm sure you miss them, Debi. I know what it's like to want to be with people who love you and not be able to be with them. I'm so sorry your parents had to leave you."

And now something really strange happens. Debi reaches down and takes my hand. Her hand is plump, dry, and chapped. Other than the baths Mom gives me, or an occasional pat from Paul or Cindy, hardly anyone ever touches me. I can't do high fives or shake hands or give hugs, and people usually don't give them to me. They don't ever realize that I might like to be touched.

Debi's hand feels warm.

I'm guessing that everyone needs to touch and be touched by others every once in a while.

23

Saturday morning. Paul, Ally, Cindy, and Tim are taking Rusty for a walk over in Discovery Park, just a couple miles from our house. Needless to say, I am not invited.

But that's okay, because Mom is driving Debi and me to McDonald's—it's Debi's reward day. Mom's always been as good as her word, and when she promised Debi a McDonald's lunch after the 911 fiasco, she meant it.

Mom parks our van in a handicapped parking space, right by the front entry to McDonald's. Debi unbuckles her seat belt and slowly opens the passenger door. She swings her legs out, glancing back at Mom and me. "I like it," she says. Both Mom and I know what she means by "it."

Mom unloads me, wheelchair and all, from the van,

and asks Debi, "Can you go ahead of us and hold the door open, please?"

Debi looks confused. "I . . . no."

Mom says, "That's okay, Debi, just go on in—we'll follow you."

Debi walks to the door and pulls it open to start to walk through, when she seems to suddenly understand what Mom asked a moment ago. "S-S-S-Swan first," she says, and holds the door open.

I can hear the smile in Mom's voice. "That's very nice of you, Debi, thank you."

Debi says, "Welcome."

It's a little past one o'clock and the restaurant is not very crowded. We get in line behind just one other customer.

At first my eyes don't focus on anything nearby. This happens a lot. You could put the most beautiful girl in the world right in front of me in a teensy string bikini—oops, that would be my brother's girlfriend—never mind. Let's say you could put the most delicious deluxe bacon double cheeseburger smack-dab, twelve inches in front of my face when I was starving. But if my eyes were focused on something outside the window, like a big piece of driftwood three miles away on Puget Sound, there'd be nothing I could do but wait until my eyes shifted.

Now my eyes do refocus. I see the counter kids in their McDonald's uniforms and the cooks behind them by the big grill. Finally I focus on the guy right in front of us in line.

Even from the back, I recognize him instantly. Long hair, black clothes, and black motorcycle boots. His name is Adam, and my brother almost killed him in our front yard last summer.

I flash back to that moment: Two bullies picking on me, this big kid Adam and his friend who lit a cigarette lighter under my chin; then Paul attacked them. Blood, gasoline, Paul's rage, and violence—it's like it all happened five minutes ago.

Fear pounds at my temples. Will Adam finish doing to me now what he and his friend started before? Paul isn't here. There's no one to stop this kid from hurting me. Mom and Debi can't do anything. I can only pray that he doesn't see me, or doesn't remember that day.

A girl at the counter brings a tray of food for him and says, "Thanks for coming to McDonald's. Have a nice day."

"Thanks," he says. He picks up the tray and turns to go to a table. The instant he sees me, I know that he recognizes me too. He freezes in his tracks. His eyes quickly scan the room, most likely to see if Paul is here with us.

I can't make myself not look at him. I can't do *anything* but wait to see what he'll do next. A buzz pounds through my brain, fear, adrenaline, anger, and disgust at my helplessness. It's weird, but I feel more scared now than the night I was alone with my dad and he held that pillow in his hands, deciding my fate, life or death.

As my eyes shift away from Adam's face, he quickly gathers himself together and pushes past us, slightly bumping his shoulder against my mom's arm.

"'Scuse me," he mumbles quickly to Mom.

Mom has no idea who this kid even is. "No problem," she says.

"I like Happy Deal," Debi says.

"Happy Meal?" Mom asks.

"Yeth," Debi repeats, "Happy Deal."

Mom smiles and says, "Okay," and orders our food.

I can't turn to see if Adam's here with his friend, can't see if I'm in danger again.

Mom wheels me over to a booth, pushing my wheelchair up snug against the table. Debi slides in. Adam is off to the side of me at his table. When I finally catch a glimpse of him, I see that he is alone. Our name is called from the counter and Mom goes back to pick up our order.

Finally my head turns fully and I focus on Adam again. He stares straight into my eyes. I feel scared, try to search for what he is thinking, try to know whether I'm in danger.

Something amazing happens. As our eyes meet, I see as clearly as anything I've ever seen his embarrassment and guilt. It's in the way his shoulders slouch down and in his sad expression. In the way his eyes keep glancing away and his face blushes. It's like I can hear his mind and feel what he wishes he could say to me: "I'm sorry for picking on you that day. I'm sorry for what we did. I'm sorry." His eyes tell me everything I need to know—that I'm safe and that I have nothing more to fear from him.

I've never realized this before, but people connect all the time, in a million different ways. Although Adam may never know it, he and I have just connected. He's spoken to me without words, saying something that words couldn't say any better.

I can't react. But if I could, I'd tell him I forgive him, that we all make mistakes and that it's pretty cool of him to feel sorry—even if he can't find the courage to speak the words out loud.

I think back to that guy in the black pickup truck who road-raged at Mom and me. Maybe he got caught up in an emotion and didn't take the time to think about our feelings. Maybe if he had seen my eyes or had a way to see all that Mom does for me, he would have stopped and felt some compassion. Maybe at some other time, in some other place, he'd be an okay guy like this kid Adam is right now. Maybe if he saw me in a pharmacy, heard me yelling "Ahhhhhhh" and glanced over, maybe his face, his eyes, and the way he looked would say, "It's okay kid, yell all you want—you should see me drive!"

Debi interrupts my thoughts. "I hun'ry," she says,

staring at her Happy Meal box.

"That's good, Debi," Mom says, unwrapping Debi's hamburger. "Eat up."

"Yeth," Debi says. "Are you hun'ry too, boyfrien'?"

"Boyfriend!" I scream inside, hoping no one has heard this and assumed that Debi and I are hooked up. It must be that when Debi can pry herself away from *The Sound of the Music,* she watches some kinda hip TV garbage—*boyfriend!!*

Mom slips a French fry into my mouth. It's salty and warm and delicious, and it instantly soothes my mental outburst. Mom rakes her fingers through my hair, and when I happen to gaze at her, the heavenly French fry juice dribbling down my chin, she smiles. "Why should Paul be the only one who gives you treats?"

I chew involuntarily, more like mash stuff around with both my tongue and my teeth. As I munch on my first tiny piece of hamburger, I think again, "Boyfriend!?" I wish I could tell Mom, "New rule: No more MTV for Debi!"

24

It's much later in the day, nighttime, and I'm sitting in my wheelchair and Debi comes and stands near me again. She takes my hand and holds it. We look out the window.

There are two boats, their running lights sparkling against the dark water.

"Purtty," Debi says, like she said last time.

"Yep," I answer silently.

We are quiet.

"You smart, S-S-S-Swan, but nobody know."

What? What did she just say?

"Nobody know you smart . . . nobody know us, S-S-S-Swan, just us know us—you know me . . . I know you."

I can't be hearing this right. She can't be saying what I'm hearing her say.

But now she adds, "You love A-A-A-Ally, but she love B-B-B-Baul."

I feel myself blush.

Debi says, "It okay, you sad but it okay."

How does Debi know all this? How does she know how I feel?

Suddenly a rush of images races through my mind: Debi staring at me so intently that day when Rusty first came. How she sits quietly so often, watching all of us, listening and staring. I always assumed that Debi didn't understand anything. I, of all people, should have known better. Just like everybody in the world "knows" how much of a veg I am, right? Debi was paying attention to the things most of us can't even see. And she was paying attention to me.

Debi mumbles, still whispering, "Wusty smart like us."

Mom walks into the room and says, "Hi, Debi, are you visiting with Shawn?"

"Yeth," Debi answers.

Mom says, "That's nice. What are you two talking about?"

Debi says, very softly, "Wusty."

"Pardon me?" Mom asks.

Debi is silent, just like always, acting as if she doesn't understand Mom's question.

Rusty, who has been lying near us on the floor this entire time, perks up at the sound of his name, his ears rising as he looks over at Debi and me. He gets up and slowly ambles over to the foot of my wheelchair, and now he plops back down, lying on his side.

Mom says, "Well, you guys have a nice chat." She leaves the room.

Debi is silent again for a while. At last she speaks. "Wusty 'n' me love you, S-S-S-Swan."

"Thanks," I think.

Debi says, louder than she has been speaking, "See you soon, S-S-S-Swan."

I wish I could nod my head and say, "Okay," but I can't. And, truthfully, I don't understand what Debi's trying to say. Doesn't she see me right now? She'll see me soon? What does she mean?

25

Okay, let's get real, and this is *not* me going into whiner mode again, it's just stating simple facts: I'll never graduate from high school, not really. Special education students at my level of disability don't actually finish required classes, but we get to hang around until we reach twenty-one, and then, whether we've learned anything or not, we have to leave. I'll never have a first love affair, first time driving a car, first time getting drunk, first time—anything. I won't go to college. I won't sky dive. I won't become a gourmet cook. I won't get married and have kids and argue with my wife. I won't get a job. Or get fired from a job. Or buy a house. Or move anyplace cool or move anyplace not cool, anytime ever. At least not until Mom dies or gets too sick or too old to take care of me anymore. And then I suppose I'll be sent somewhere else to live. Like Debi was sent to us. What will happen to me is whatever life brings next. And in this way, I'm like everyone else.

But here's something I've also figured out. Maybe my ideas about being known and knowing others are a little bit off. I thought I knew Rusty. I thought I knew Debi. I wasn't even close. I know that I'm smart. Debi is supposedly stupid and Rusty's a dog. Yet they both figured me out. Maybe it's because this whole business of knowing someone and being known by them is different than I've thought. Maybe my assumptions based on how "normal" people, even my own family, treat me have led me down the wrong path. There's a lot I still don't know. But if Debi and Rusty and I can all connect more deeply, what does that say about how we can connect with everyone else?

It's been a while since Debi told me she knows I'm smart. Now, whenever I see her sitting and staring, I know what's really going on. She is gathering info about Mom, Cindy, Paul, and Ally. It's amazing to feel understood by her and to want to understand her in return.

I'm sitting in my regular spot in my wheelchair by the window when a seagull flies past, low, gliding. It's dark gray, with hardly any speckles at all. Watching it, I think about how much this seagull's gliding flight reminds me of when my spirit escapes my body. I start to think, "Maybe some-day after I die, I'll get to come back as a seagull, a beautiful, gray ghost bird soaring." I laugh inside my mind, thinking, "No, given my luck, I'll probably return as a fly or cockroach."

Debi, who is across the room, laughs. She says, "S-S-S-Swan funny."

Mom asks Debi, "You mean Shawn's arms?"

Debi says, "He funny."

Mom says, "Shawn's arm movements just happen to him sometimes—he doesn't do it to be funny."

"No," Debi insists. "He funny inside . . . good funny."

Mom nods.

Arm movements? I didn't realize that my arms were moving, flopping about like wings trying to lift me up as I was thinking about flying. I had never put the two things together, that my body was actually working in connection with my brain.

Debi says; "S-S-S-Swan funny lotta times . . . funny t'ings inside."

Mom asks, "You mean you have funny thoughts about Shawn?"

I scream silently, "No, Mom, inside ME! Debi means that my thoughts are funny, things that I think about, that's what she is saying! She understands me!"

Debi smiles but remains silent. Mom doesn't say anything more either.

* * *

106

Debi has changed things for our whole family. Despite her handicaps, or maybe because of them, she shows us daily that her feelings and thoughts are real. It's not that Debi loves me more than Mom or Cindy or Paul do. She simply has time to focus, while others, so-called normal people, are always rushing about and tend to see things only on the surface.

It's not that the other people in my life are self-absorbed. They aren't—my mom especially. But they've simply never been trapped in their own bodies. They've never been seen by everyone else as unaware and lost in themselves. From their perspective, there isn't much reason to believe that I'm highly functioning in here. But what if Mom and Cindy and Paul—anyone who is paying attention—could see my wheels turning for just a moment from a look in my eyes, or wonder if my arm movement might be connected to something I was thinking? I wonder what they'd feel. I know this probably won't ever happen. . . . Then again, never say never.

26

I **am lying in my bed, waiting for Mom to come** get me up. It's Sunday morning, so there's no big rush to feed, bathe, and dress me.

A seizure starts. I relax and let it carry me away.

I arrive in a room, an unfamiliar room, and in the dark shadows of the corner is the figure, the one who keeps showing up in my dreams. The figure has no clear outline of the body, as if it's wearing a cloak or huge coat made of darkness, but for the first time I sense that this figure is a woman. She is not menacing. I don't believe she means me any harm. It's hard to explain, but since she has joined me, I've been pulled away from the absolute freedom I've had in my dream and spirit journeys. At first I was scared, then frustrated. Now I'm not angry or sad or even confused. Maybe excited. I think she has a purpose. I just don't know what it is. If she wanted to hurt me, she'd have done it by now. If she doesn't care about me, why does she keep coming back? I'm not scared of her anymore.

I ask, "Who are you? Why are you showing up in my world?"

She stays silent. But that's going to change. After all, these are *my* dreams, *my* spirit travels, and I have a right to know what's going on.

27

It's the next morning, Monday. Something weird is happening, something different. I feel it under my skin, a strange tingly feeling—I can't explain it, but something is off.

For one thing, Rusty acts as crazy as he did the first day he came here.

Debi finished making her lunch and putting the dishes from the dishwasher away sooner than normal and went to sit on the bench and wait for her bus. Maybe she didn't give Rusty his regular morning treat? If that's what his nutty behavior is about, this dog better plan on a visit to the Betty Ford Doggy Addiction Clinic for Milk-Bone Junkies, because he's driving me crazy.

Rusty sits right in front of Debi, barking and whining. Mom calls, "Hey, Debi, tell Rusty to cool it."

Debi doesn't answer. Nothing new.

Mom yells a bit louder, "Rusty, hush! Debi, pay attention please!" Still no answer from Debi.

Seriously Debi, do you have eardrums of steel? She must be in one of her zones.

"Paul," Mom calls, "will you get Rusty? I need some peace and quiet."

Paul brings a heaping tablespoon full of Honey Nut Cheerios to his mouth and while chewing yells, "Rusty, come here."

Rusty ignores Paul and keeps barking.

Paul looks up, stops eating, and commands "Rusty, knock it off. *Come!*"

Rusty stops barking but continues to whine and still doesn't come to Paul.

"Dammit," Paul snaps, dropping his spoon so that it clanks loudly as it hits the side of his bowl. He gets up from the table.

"Take it easy, Paul," Mom says.

Paul says, "I'm not gonna hurt him, Mom, but he needs to obey."

Paul walks through the kitchen and into the living room. I can hear him clearly because Rusty's whining gets softer, almost like whimpering, as Paul approaches.

"Rusty, come," Paul commands again. From my spot in my wheelchair in the kitchen, I don't hear Rusty's claws clacking on the hardwood floor.

Paul says, "Debi, what's up? Why's your dog so—" He stops in mid-sentence. "Debi?" Paul speaks her name in a totally different tone of voice, soft, and now again in that same tone, "Debi? You okay?" There is another brief pause.

"Mom, come here. Hurry." Paul sounds scared.

I snap to full attention.

"Mom," Paul cries again.

Mom and Cindy both hurry to the living room, and I hear Mom, her voice as scared and worried as Paul's, "Debi . . . Debi darling . . . Debi."

Cindy says, "Oh God, is she—"

Mom ignores Cindy and says to Paul, "Help me get Debi down onto the floor."

Rusty barks, frantic, terrified, threatening barks.

Paul says, "No, Rusty, sit—*sit*. Cindy, grab his collar and hold him back."

I hear a soft thump sound and Mom saying all the time, "Debi . . . Debi . . . sweetie . . ." She says, "Paul, call 911. I'll try CPR."

Paul hurries back to the kitchen. He picks up the phone and pushes the buttons. His face is pale and his hand holding the phone seems to be quivering. In a matter of seconds he speaks. "Our . . . our cousin is unconscious . . . I think she's . . . we need an ambulance. . . ." He listens for a few moments and calls, "Mom, can you feel a pulse?"

112

Mom yells back, "No."

Paul continues talking to the 911 person, tells his name, our address. I hear all his words, but none of them matter much. I'm worried about Debi.

Mom continues doing CPR.

Paul, after hanging up the phone, goes back and holds on to Rusty. Paul whispers, "It's okay, buddy, it's okay," but Rusty keeps whining.

The ambulance arrives a few minutes later, along with a fire engine and several police cars. The paramedics quickly check Debi's vitals and take over the CPR.

After what seems like a long time, one of the paramedics finally says to his partner, "She's flat-lined."

"Yep," says the other one. "You wanna call it?"

"Yeah. Cardiac arrest, I bet. So many Down syndrome patients go this way."

The other paramedic stands and turns to my family, who are all watching from the doorway. "I'm sorry," he says, "she's gone."

"Gone?"

He means Debi is dead.

28

The following Saturday, I do not go to Debi's funeral. The rest of my family—even Dad, who only met Debi once—is there. I am at home with a caregiver who has parked me in front of the window while she watches TV. I try to force myself not to feel angry, but I am. I know everyone thinks I'm a veg, and usually I can handle that. But not today.

I try to rationalize, talk myself down. Nobody believes I have a brain inside me that connects to my heart. Nobody knows that I understand anything about anything—only Debi knew that. So why would someone drag my wheelchair across the soggy grass of a cemetery just so that I can sit next to a hole in the ground as Debi is laid to rest in her grave, like I've seen on TV funerals a million times? If I have no brain, I can't grieve. Right? If I have no understanding of anything, why should I be someplace where everyone else is sad?

But these rationalizations don't help much today. I am angry that Debi died. I am mad that I don't get to say good-bye, even in my own way, even if no one knows I'm saying it except me. I'm upset that other people can make such important decisions for me, and that they have no way of knowing that I am *not* utterly, incalculably, irretrievably stupid. They don't know how sad I feel.

Debi understood the way my heart and brain work; she understood my life, *me*, better than anyone else ever has.

Rusty didn't get to go to the funeral either. All morning long he whines and whimpers, and walks back and forth in front of my wheelchair. Finally he sits down at my feet and stares at me. He lifts his paw gently into my lap, leaves it there awhile, then takes it away and rubs his body against my legs. I'm sure he's leaving tons of dog hair all over me, but I don't care, because let's be honest, I'm not much of a fashion king anyway.

Tears roll down my cheeks—it feels good and awful and painful all at the same time.

The reception following Debi's service is here at the house. Mom and Cindy and Paul get home first, followed only a few minutes later by Dad. Mrs. Pearson, Debi's caseworker who brought her here for that first visit, and Jack Yurrik, who brought Rusty, soon arrive. Rusty is banished to the backyard as people I've never met begin to trickle in.

Many of these people are classmates from Debi's Learning Skills Program. They walk right past me with shoulders slumped, some with mouths agape. Several of the men wear neckties with huge, awkward-looking knots, and a number of the ladies are in inappropriate dresses, pink or bright sunflower yellow or faded prints. And all these special needs guests wear shoes that are held on their feet with Velcro straps, just like Debi's used to be, just like mine still are.

A number of Debi's friends from "schoo" surround the food in the dining room and load up their plates. A few of them jibber-jabber on, while others stand quietly, looking confused as they eat and avoid conversations.

There is little talk of Debi. Sitting in my wheelchair in my regular spot, I listen for anyone to say something kind or caring or even some neutral comment about Debi's life.

No one does.

29

When the last of the guests is gone, Paul brings Rusty back into the house. Since Debi's death, Rusty has been more subdued. When Rusty and Paul used to play, Rusty would get this excited look in his eyes. And I swear his mouth would curl up just like he was grinning from ear to ear. Since Debi's been gone, I haven't seen Rusty smile once.

Cindy starts carrying little plates and silverware to the sink, and Mom begins rinsing them and loading them into the dishwasher.

Paul asks, "How can I help?"

Mom answers, "When Cindy is through cleaning up, will you put the folding chairs back in the storage room downstairs?" Mom's voice sounds so sad, tired, and beaten.

"Sure," Paul says, sitting in the dining room and petting

Rusty, who lies at his feet nudging up against him.

After a moment, Cindy says, "I guess that was a nice service, but—"

"But what?" Mom asks.

At first Cindy hesitates. "I don't know how to say it, but somehow it's like Debi passing away isn't as sad as when someone normal dies. I know this sounds mean, I just—I don't know how to put it."

Paul says, "I know. It's weird. I guess when you think about her life, you have to wonder, what more was there for her to do?"

Mom turns off the faucet and pauses. Paul looks worried for a moment.

"Mom, are we awful?" he asks.

"No," Mom answers. "Maybe what you are saying could be twisted to sound heartless, but I know that's not how you mean it." Mom motions Cindy and Paul to come closer. "None of us like to think about it, or acknowledge it, but we live in a world, a society anyway, that gives a material value to everything and everybody. How much money do you make? How rich and famous are you? We put a value on everyone's life and thus on everyone's death."

Paul says, "I know. It's such bull. Pro sports figures and movie stars get paid huge bucks, and everyone treats the rich and famous like they're better than everyone else."

Cindy says, "Not everyone who is famous is rich and glamorous."

Paul looks at Cindy and waits for her to explain.

Cindy says, "I Googled 'Shawn McDaniel' the other day."

Paul smiles. "How'd the big boy do?"

Cindy says, "For just Shawn McDaniel, 4,770,000. For Shawn McDaniel and the word poetry, 310,000 and for 'Shawn McDaniel' in quotes and the name of Dad's book, *Shawn*, 119,800."

Paul says, "Not too shabby."

Cindy says, "I know—thanks to Dad's poem, Shawn's famous."

Mom adds, "Your brother being born brain injured led your dad to write his story. And his book has changed so many people's attitudes and feelings toward kids like Shawn."

Paul interjects, "And made Dad a rich big shot."

Mom says, "Your dad would trade everything for your brother to be okay."

Paul doesn't hesitate. "I know."

Sitting in my wheelchair across the room, listening to all of this, I know that everything they are saying is true. Except the part about my Google fame. Maybe thousands, tens of thousands, even millions of people know my name, know that I exist. Maybe they even think they know me through reading my dad's writings about me. But they don't know who I am, or even that I'm really in here. Sure, my being born brain damaged, and my dad writing about it, changed a lot of peoples' attitudes toward kids like me. But the only person who has ever really known me was Debi.

30

All my efforts to understand and rationalize to myself why my life is worthwhile, all my Gee-Ain't-Life-Grand Cool Things About Being ME, seem so stupid right now. As idiotic as thinking I was in love with Ally. As crazy as thinking anyone could truly connect with me.

In addition to missing the funeral, I never got to go near Debi before they covered her up and lifted her onto a gurney and rolled her away. I didn't get to look at her, or say good-bye. She is the first dead person I've ever known. I mean, the first person I knew who had been alive but now is dead. Even my grandparents are still living, although I hardly ever see them.

I can't shake my feeling of sadness. But it's even more than that—more like hopelessness.

Crackle-crackle-crackle . . . I feel a seizure coming on. A soft laugh comes out as electrical current pulses through my head. I choke a little, gasping and gagging as the muscles in my throat tighten, constricting my breathing—here I go again. . . .

I am sitting in a room, the same empty room where I last saw the dark figure. This time the room is bright and I feel comfortable. There are two chairs, the one on which I'm sitting and an empty one directly across from me. A door opens, and for a second or two no one steps through it. But now the dark figure comes into the room. I've never seen her this close before. I can almost see her features, her face.

"Hi," I say.

"Hello," I hear back from her. A familiar female voice, though I can't quite place it.

"Nice to finally meet you," I say.

"You've known me all along," she answers, a soft laugh in her words.

"I'm Shawn," I say in my mind to her.

She answers, "Yes, Shawn."

Just as I'm ready to ask, "What's your name?" the figure laughs again and throws off her darkness, sitting down in the chair right across from me. There is a glow, a shimmering outline all around her. I can't believe what I'm seeing, feeling, thinking, *knowing*.

"Debi?" I ask.

"Yes, Shawn," she says again. Not "yeth," not "S-S-S-Swan," but "Yes, Shawn," clear and happy, her voice full of joy.

31

I stare into Debi's eyes and she looks back—we don't speak, we don't need to, as I can feel her thoughts and I know she feels mine.

I wonder, why did I see Debi as a dark figure before? I realize that maybe it wasn't Debi that was the dark figure at all—no, not maybe, it definitely wasn't. It was my sense of her, my thoughts about who she was then. Debi had no meanness in her, no cruelty, no darkness, I supplied all of that.

I think about Debi dying yet being here with me now. I wonder, what difference does it make whether she is dead or alive. I start to answer, "All the difference in the world," but I stop myself. I don't know the answer to this—maybe nobody does. None of us know what happens when we leave our bodies behind. But our spirits are the purest parts of ourselves; alive, dead, good, bad, one chromosome too many or a few too few, these matters don't matter to your soul. Like everyone else, I tell myself what is real and what isn't. I use words like *life*, *death*, *heaven*, *hell*, talking as if I knew what these things are, but none of us *really* know—

Now a larger thought overwhelms me. Not just a thought—a feeling, a hope, something more important than anything else: I'm alive, and I'm here to learn, to live and to know and to be known. I think maybe that's what love is all about, and it's all that matters.

All these thoughts have come at once, in the length of two heartbeats. Debi still sits across from me, sharing all of it. I want to ask her how she likes the freedom of leaving her body behind, a freedom I've treasured so much for so long.

But Debi sighs and says, "I have to go, Shawn—I love you."

I say, "I love you, too."

She hesitates, pauses for just a moment, and smiles. "See you later," she says.

As Debi begins to disappear, fading into soft light, I feel my seizure racing to an end. I wish we could stay together longer. . . . I wish we could talk about our lives: What do they mean? Why are we here? Why were we born the way we are? Why . . . ?

* * *

Back in my body again. Rusty lies on the floor at the foot of my wheelchair. He stares up at me intently, as though he knows exactly what I've just been through.

The wind outside the window moves the branches of the trees and the small leaves quiver lightly on those branches, as if they are waving to the world. I stare at the tree, a thick trunk, big and small branches, shimmering leaves. And for the first time ever, I think about its unseen roots, spreading out into the earth below—hidden and invisible, but every bit as important as all the rest of the tree.

My gaze shifts to Rusty again. He smiles.

I think silently to him, "I know, boy."

He drops his head back down and sighs. I don't feel like sighing. I'm more alive than I've ever been before.

32

There once was a guy who, when he'd dream, could never tell if he was a man or a butterfly—I think I know what he felt like. What's a dream and what's real? In the end, it seems to me that we are made up of both our dreams and our waking selves. All of us dream and then wake up, only to dream and awaken again, over and over all through our lives.

Life is always about what happens next, or at least that's what we feel while we're busy living it. But what happens next is always just more life; crazy, funny, sad, hopeless, hopeful, winning, losing, being known but never being fully known.

In my bed tonight, as I lie here waiting for sleep, I think about everything, but mostly about the people who already love me. I know that they don't know me, don't know who I really am under my skin and inside. But nobody ever *really* knows *anyone* else. We are looks and brains, bodies and faces that we show to the world. But appearance and brains and even our bodies are only a part of us. It's our souls and spirits that live on forever.

I think about the ending of Dad's poem "Shawn":

I hold Shawn tenderly.

In sleep, voice quiet,

He breathes.

Hands still, in silence, slumbering,

His spirit is a feather on a quiet river.

His person, his being, some kind of impossible, painful,

Incomprehensible gift.

Even though my dad felt this way about me when he wrote his poem, he ran away instead of finding some way for us to connect. My father could never see me. I wish I could tell him what I believe, that our souls are forever linked, that we'll always be together, whether he knows this or not.

Rusty saw and protected me and Debi befriended me. If

Debi with all her so-called "handicaps" and "disabilities" saw me for who I am and found me inside my broken self, who's to say that someday, someone else won't see me too? Who's to say that even my dad might not one day overcome his fears and find me? I'm not just my body. And I'm not anyone else's beliefs about who I am.

I'm Shawn McDaniel. I love and am loved. I'm alive and happy. Thanks to my dad's poem "Shawn," a lot of people think they know me. But I hope that someday I'll meet someone who will know me as much as I want to be known, someone who sees that I am not just my limitations. My future doesn't have to be what my life looks like right now. What's next for me? What happens now? All I know for sure is that life happens next. How cool is that?

Author's Note

It's not possible to tell all that has happened in the life of my son Sheehan Trueman, a profoundly developmentally disabled man. Or in the life of *Stuck in Neutral* after it was selected as a Printz Honor Book in January 2001 and how the book has touched so many people, including those with developmental disabilities and their care providers. Or the ways my life has changed on account of having written Shawn's story.

In 2001 I remarried. Patti and I had already been together for nearly a decade with the shared responsibility of providing care in our home for her younger sister Donna, who has Down syndrome.

My invention of Debi Eagen in this story is based on the life of my sister-in-law Donna, just as Shawn McDaniel is based on my son Sheehan. Shawn and Debi are fictional creations. *I made them up.* But it's unlikely I'd ever have been able to invent and create such characters without being a part of Sheehan's and Donna's real lives.

My stories are an attempt to expand my readers' and my own compassion, empathy, and understanding of the lives of people struggling and dealing with extraordinary challenges and situations. I hope this sequel to *Stuck in Neutral* achieves that higher purpose.

Terry Trueman

Acknowledgments

Readers of this novel while a work in progress include: Stephanie Squicciarrini, Stacie Wachholz, Kelly Milner Halls, Anne Wright, Sherri Fulton, Shelley Whaley, Carol Plum-Ucci, Dr. William Britt, Beth Cooley, Richard Higgerson, Terry John Pratt, Cindy Trueman, Bob, Debbie, and Brianna Cole, Katelyn "Traeh" Putnam. Special thanks to Mark McVeigh, my agent for this book, whose initial enthusiasm and support for a sequel to *Stuck in Neutral* helped me find the courage to write it, and whose editorial ideas made it so much better. My first editor at HarperCollins, Antonia Markiet, helped me shape the original *Stuck in Neutral* and *Cruise Control* (and four other novels); my agent George Nicholson at Sterling Lord Literistic, Inc., put those first novels into Antonia's hands. Thanks to Jayne Carapezzi and later Jessica MacLeish, who helped with much of this work. Phoebe Yeh was primary editor on *Life Happens Next*, and her guidance and brilliance are impossible to exaggerate. Susan Katz, Kate Morgan Jackson, and many other people at HC made this book possible. Family and friends: Patti, Jesse, Sheehan, Donna, the real Rusty (aka Rusty Shackelford), and many additional usual suspects including teachers, librarians, and fellow authors helped too. Hopefully you all know who you are, and I apologize for not naming everyone individually.

★ "An intense reading experience."
–ALA *Booklist* (starred review)

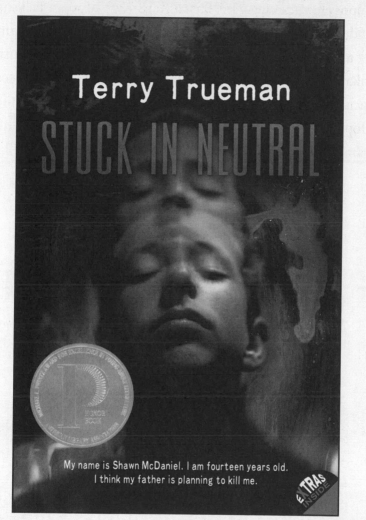

Terry Trueman

STUCK IN NEUTRAL

HONOR BOOK

My name is Shawn McDaniel. I am fourteen years old.
I think my father is planning to kill me.

EXTRAS INSIDE

A Michael L. Printz Honor Book

HARPER TEEN
n Imprint of HarperCollins*Publishers*

www.epicreads.com

7/13, 12/14, 9/15